⫸ **P9-APS-282**

Despite her careful upbringing, the rigid instructions as to propriety, she was no stranger to kisses. But most admirers had been hesitant, timid, not sure of the passion they thought they had read on her smiling lips when she teased them. If too much passion was shown, or possessiveness beyond her personal desires, she invariably ended the matter with a cool setdown. Few clumsy admirers were proof against that.

Stephen Kyle, however, gave her no time to demonstrate her control of the embrace. His lips brushed hers in a titillating way that made her shiver pleasurably. When she would have broken away to taunt him or play the shocked maiden his hand held the lower half of her face in a vise, and his mouth captured hers again. She responded with a passion she had never known before, and for a few seconds she was happier than she had ever been. . . .

BOOK HOUSE
New & Used Paper Backs
692 Puckett Dr.
Mableton, Ga. 30059
944-3275

Fawcett Crest Books
by Ann Stanfield:

THE DOXY MASQUE

THE GOLDEN MARGUERITE

ROYAL SUMMER

THE
DOXY
MASQUE

Ann Stanfield

FAWCETT CREST • NEW YORK

A Fawcett Crest Book
Published by Ballantine Books
Copyright © 1986 by Virginia Coffman

All rights reserved under International and Pan-American Copyright Conventions. Published in the United States by Ballantine Books, a division of Random House, Inc., New York, and simultaneously in Canada by Random House of Canada Limited, Toronto.

Library of Congress Catalog Card Number: 86-91188

ISBN: 0-449-20996-2

All the characters in this book are fictitious, and any resemblance to persons living or dead is purely coincidental.

Manufactured in the United States of America

First Edition: December 1986

CHAPTER ONE

Lady Favia Dalreagh returned early that afternoon to the fashionable house she and her mother had taken for the Brighton Season.

Favia had shortened her first shopping expedition of the Season out of annoyance with the subject of Stephen Kyle, only to hear her mother's languid voice bewailing the man whose name had driven Favia from the shops.

"That odious creature! One wonders why His Highness troubles to receive him. They do say Stephen Spencer Kyle is a confirmed liberal. I shall give him the merest nod if he comes in my way. I am persuaded Favia will have the good sense to cut him. They met once in Bath, you know."

Favia smiled wryly at that. She may have met Mr. Stephen Spencer Kyle eight years ago at a Subscription Ball in Bath, but the Member of Parliament could not be said to have "met" her. He merely turned his handsome, arrogant head, looking through the nervous young lady and, having bowed politely in response to the introduction by the Master of Ceremonies, he walked away.

"Well, my disdainful friend, I shall certainly make you remember me this time," Lady Favia promised herself now as she started up the elegant white staircase. There was a glitter in her celebrated periwinkle-blue eyes that might have warned the gentleman, if he took the time to observe her at all.

In the open gallery above the stairs her mother, the Countess of Dalreagh, gossiped with the busy housekeeper, Mrs. Natterby, who nodded agreeably to all the countess's opinions while she directed the upstairs maid to sweep out of and not into corners.

The countess, a slender little woman of deceptively fragile and faded beauty, saw Favia and dismissed Mrs. Natterby without a second's thought.

"Ah, there you are, Favia dearest! Do come in to my sitting room and let us have a comfortable gossip. I've been wretched all morning. Not a soul to bear me company. I was forced to send that dreary Miss Durrance out to match some silks for my petit-point screen and to return those books of mine. However, I should have recalled that she spends forever at Clackett's Library. I cannot imagine what has detained her this time. Heaven knows, it shouldn't be that difficult to exchange two novels for me. Have you read Mrs. Radcliffe's latest, *Children of the Forest*? Or do I mean *The Abbey*? Some such flummery."

"Yes, Mother. How are you feeling? You look very well."

The countess stiffened. "That's as may be. I assure you I have never felt less well. I stooped to pick up some of my floss that Durrance carelessly let fall, and my poor head seemed to spin. You will not credit this, but it was only with the greatest effort that I could persuade her to exert herself and fetch me those silk threads I need in town. Said she had the headache. Oh, she smiled and smiled, but one could see she was reluctant. And I've

2

wanted those threads this age. She has the most remarkable talent for idleness.''

''Really? I hadn't noticed it.'' The luckless Adelaide Durrance was the countess's fourth companion in a year.

Favia suspected that hired companions were merely a symptom of her mother's real problem. Though her late husband's cousin, Martin Dalreagh, had succeeded to the earl's title three years before, he was unmarried and the countess remained the only woman possessing her particular title.

The countess had removed with Favia to the charming Tudor cottage called the Dalreagh Dower House in a pretty glade back of Dalreagh Hall, but when the new earl entertained, it was she, the genuine Countess of Dalreagh, who played hostess. The blow had fallen last year, in the exciting celebrations after Waterloo, when the new earl discovered Miss Elfreda Worthingham, daughter of a Whig politician, very plump in the pockets, and a marriage was arranged.

The dreaded marriage day was put off until the spring of 1816, but the hour was almost at hand, and within a fortnight the true countess would become that hated title, ''Dowager Countess'' while Miss Elfreda Worthingham, odious, commonplace name!—would supersede her as Countess of Dalreagh.

It was enough to give anyone the vapors, the countess complained to Favia, who laughed at her prejudice but secretly found herself sharing it. Elfreda Worthingham was maddeningly officious. However, there was little doubt that she meant well.

There was still a painful time to be gotten over. Favia knew that she and her mother would attend the Dalreagh wedding. It was to be a private affair with the ceremony taking place in the old, disused chapel of the estate, but

3

the absence of Favia and the Dowager Countess would have been an unforgivable affront.

Poor Mama! There was little to be said that would console her, but at least, there were several days before they need return to Wiltshire for the "celebrations."

Favia took her mother's arm and drew her into the pretty pink sitting room that adjoined the regal bedchamber the countess had chosen for her own.

The countess seated herself on the pale pink, silk-tufted chaise between the two sunny windows and arranged the flowing lengths of her primrose morning gown gracefully around her form.

"Now, draw up that footstool and sit here before me. Tell me what they are saying in town about the Regent's Masquerade tonight. Do they actually expect that dreadful Mr. Kyle to attend after all the horrid things he has said in Commons about His Highness? This Kyle person is much admired by the Worthinghams. All Whig reformers, you know. You may imagine what sort of man he is if Elfreda Worthingham calls him a friend. I daresay, tonight he will appear as the devil himself."

Favia pulled up the petit-point–covered stool and seated herself tentatively.

"Mother, Elfreda isn't the only one who seems to have taken a fancy to Mr. Kyle. I discovered this morning that other females invited to His Highness's Pavilion do not share your abhorrence for the man. Despite his politics and his indifference to royalty, Mr. Kyle seems to have aroused interest among your precious beau monde. I heard nothing but talk of him in every milliner's shop, every mercer's rooms, down North Street. A great bore, I do assure you."

The countess raised her head, tilted it on one side, and studied Favia like a bright-eyed bird.

4

"Is he, my dear?"

"Is he what?"

"A boring subject to you, this Stephen Spencer Kyle?"

Favia avoided her eyes and turned her attention to the sunlit waters beyond the window.

"I have no interest in him, one way or the other."

"That is a relief, at all events."

But Favia was remembering with all the old bitterness and disappointment that first meeting with the elusive Mr. Kyle, if one could call it a meeting.

However captivating Stephen Kyle might be to the ladies of the Prince Regent's more impressionable circle, Favia would only admit to a mild curiosity about "what must happen tonight" when the terrible M.P. was presented to His Highness, the Regent, at the Pavilion's masquerade and reception.

But she found nothing attractive about a man who seemed to take pleasure in hindering all the proposals put forward by His Royal Highness. The Prince's politics might be more talk than action, but he did try to see the viewpoint of the less fortunate. Even Stephen Kyle must admit that the Prince Regent demonstrated more personal interest in his subjects than any of his Hanover ancestors had shown.

The countess ran a finger thoughtfully down the spotted-silk sleeve of her primrose gown. "I daresay, His Highness will show you marked attention tonight, if he recognizes you in your masquerade. He appeared to be in raptures over you at the Subscription Concert. That dreadful chatterbox, the Duchess of Hungerford, was aware of it, you may be sure. She fancied herself as his new favorite. But the fashion seems to be shifting from brunet to blond, I am happy to say; for you, my dear, are the prettiest of all His Highness's golden beauties."

"Dear Mama, let Beatrix Hungerford keep his attention.

I don't wish to be one of his golden beauties." She added firmly, "I have no intention of becoming anyone's mistress, even to oblige His Royal Highness. Forgive me now. I must change. I have calls to make." She arose and started out, pursued by her mother's plaintive call.

"Oh, Favia, why must you be forever running away? As though a few calls were more important to you than your wretched mother's loneliness."

Favia stopped in the doorway. She smiled to soften the harshness of her words. "If you would stop sending that poor Miss Durrance on errands every hour, and try not to let Elfreda or Martin offend you so often when we are home in Wiltshire, you would not be alone. As for the calls I am making, the most important is to Minta Vennor, who served you, certainly me, very faithfully for twelve years."

"Eleven and a trifle," the countess corrected her carefully. "But really, my dear, I could scarcely keep her on. It became quite impossible for the poor thing to perform the few tasks I asked of her after you grew far too old to need a governess. That appalling rheumatic conditon. Even her fingers. Such a tragedy in one so young! Scarcely my age."

"Yes, it is a tragedy. But I see no reason to add to it by avoiding her now. I shall take her flowers and some of the new novels. She still criticizes them, but she will read them all the same. They may brighten her days."

"Flowers and books cost money. And only yesterday you were scolding me about my extravagance. As though a new set of matching chairs could be called an extravagance! They weren't for my apartments, as you very well know. They are for the little blue salon in the Dower House, which is grown quite shabby."

"I know, Mother. Now, I must go. Miss Vennor is expecting me."

Favia left her mother's presence as rapidly as possible. In Favia's observation the countess had been too cosseted by her husband, who had adored his frail wife to the exclusion of all others, even his daughter. When the Earl of Dalreagh had died of a putrid throat in the huge bed he bequeathed to his widow, his beautiful but independent daughter was expected to succeed him in fulfilling her mother's slightest whim. It was difficult, though not impossible. Favia had spent much of her life putting her mother's whims before her own desires.

But as that portion of the Dalreagh fortune that was not entailed shrank to a dangerous low point, the countess's whims and expensive tastes were proving more and more difficult to fill. Favia often longed to treat her mother like a spoiled child, permitting her only half the daily trinkets and favors she demanded. However, habit was firmly engrained. Then, too, her mother's very weakness appealed to Favia's strong protective streak. The countess needed her.

Favia Dalreagh knew it was her responsibility to improve the Dalreaghs' financial situation. Although she had given it considerable thought, there seemed only two possibilities at the moment: one, that she should marry into great wealth, such as that of the Dalreaghs' neighbor, Vincent Viscount Kinsham, a gambler of some charm, some wit, and an apparently limitless fortune. A man she liked moderately and trusted not at all. The second possibility involved winning the Regent's regard and gifts of property without letting herself become the latest in a long and illustrious parade of royal mistresses.

It required some delicate maneuvering. Meanwhile, she

must change for her afternoon visit. Returning to her bedchamber, she rang for her maid.

Young Libbie Beckett, Favia's abigail, had been rescued by the countess from a mercer's shop in Bath where the girl had just snatched a reticule belonging to the beautiful, raven-haired Duchess of Hungerford. Thus far, the countess's good deed was admirable, but she had at once presented the shifty-eyed, light-fingered little creature to Favia with instructions to train her as a personal maid, since Favia's own abigail was marrying the Dalreagh family butler, having started to increase in an embarrassing way.

Because the task of reforming Libbie Beckett would be something of a challenge, and Favia thrived on challenges, she had taken the girl in hand. The girl learned rapidly, and as an abigail, she was something of a success. However, old habits died hard. Favia never knew when some trinket or bit of clothing would disappear. She had one consolation. She knew exactly where and how to recover it.

Once challenged, Libbie returned the object instantly, accompanied by an injured sniff.

"Precisely as though I had given her the wretched gloves and then reclaimed them," Favia complained to her mother. "Perhaps I should return her to you. You are at home more and can watch her."

The countess had gently refused. "She twitches, dear. And there is a furtive look about her eyes that I cannot like. My nerves would never permit it."

Favia resigned herself, until the next time. After all was said, the girl had become a reasonably efficient lady's maid.

In Favia's bedchamber Beckett had her new barred silk walking dress laid out and was looking expectant.

Favia shook her head. "Thank you, Libbie, but I won't

8

need the blue silk. I shall wear the pink sprigged muslin.'' In Favia's opinion, pink gave her a demure and simpering look quite unlike her usual sophisticated appearance. It might serve to distract attention from her true identity. "And I will take—I think—that pink silk and milan straw bonnet." This bonnet had been chosen by her mother two years ago and demonstrated the countess's taste, not her own. It was far too young, Favia thought, and not her sort.

"It isn't in the present style, ma'am. Such a deep crown. A body would think you was a parlor maid or some'ut."

"Just so."

Beckett was shocked and her small, busy eyes stared, but she obeyed. While Favia dressed, Libbie Beckett made an effort to discover more about Favia's proposed visit.

"But Your La'ship, Pitcher Street is mighty dangerous. I knew a lad—he was fly to all the latest rigs, and his ken was Pitcher Street. So, mind you, take care."

"I shall, Libbie. But Miss Vennor is a very respectable lady, I assure you. Unfortunately, she has no one to care for her and her friends must rally to her."

Beckett rolled her eyes. Friendship was not a subject that captured her interest.

Satisfied that she looked like a penniless but respectable young servant, Favia left the splendid house, one of many tightly fitted along the Steyne. She made her way over the seafront promenade among the visitors to Brighton, nodding, smiling, inclining her head to her friends, amused at the surprise over her demure appearance, which showed none of the supposed Dalreagh wealth. She suspected her "fashionable" reputation must reel under a severe blow that day. Then, too, she had walked out alone. Where was her maid, or even a male escort? Her smile had a note of impudence as she returned various greetings.

After witnessing one more startled look of recognition she sauntered inland, away from the dazzling, sunlit sea. Wishing she had taken a sunshade against the unexpected heat of the afternoon, she turned from the busy shopping thoroughfare of North Street and its environs, walking through close little streets, scarcely more than alleys, crowded with life of a very different sort from the wealth exhibited in the new shopping area made fashionable by the Prince Regent and his coterie.

Everywhere among these narrow-fronted old buildings and in the alleys between, she noticed the age, lack of care, and, saddest of all to Favia, the signs of a former, pleasant life destroyed by time and new fashions.

The house she sought was one of many huddled together here between noisome, dangerous alleys now fallen upon evil times. Miss Vennor would have been very much at home in these lodgings had they been better cared for and the neighborhood less infested with unsavory denizens.

A powerful-looking, unsavory denizen of the male variety was slinking up the nearest alley toward her. He was filthy enough to be a chimney sweep, but he wielded a woodsman's ax and apparently headed somewhere to produce firewood. He became less sinister when he reached Favia. A big grin relieved the heaviness of his dirty face, and she grinned back.

He went on about his business while she tried to mount the steps to Miss Vennor's lodging house but was impeded by two sharp-nosed old harridans who might have escaped from a London fish market. They had their heads together and were clearly discussing Favia. They caught the end of her own big grin as she turned from the man with the ax, but the women did not react as pleasantly. She heard remarks about "swells" and "them as thinks they'll cut a dash afore decent females."

She tried to show them a quiet civility but they met both her "good day" and her tentative smile with a nasty exchange of looks and a refusal to budge from their full occupation of the steps. Without losing her pleasant manner or her smile, Favia moved one of the women firmly aside with a very proper "Your pardon, ma'am" and went inside the once-respectable old house. The women seemed too surprised to make objections.

The small entry of the house still showed signs of its early eighteenth-century richness, but like the front it was uncared for. The staircase was festooned with fingerprints, and one could write a name in the dust on the carefully carved balustrade. Miss Vennor had always been so immaculate. This must distress her very much.

Minta Vennor, her tall, angular body bent like bamboo by the progress of her disease, leaned over the top of the balustrade to greet Favia, an unexpected softness warming the lines of her long face. Pressed to her flat bosom by clawlike, rheumatic hands, was the India shawl the Earl of Dalreagh had given her as a New Year's present almost ten years ago. Her frosty, gruff voice and her manner, imperious to the point of indifference, did not sway Favia, who knew her so well.

"Good evening, Lady Favia. You are looking well."

"Vennie dear, how good it is to see you, and do stop calling me 'Lady Favia.' I am the very same girl you chastised when I was naughty." Favia reached her and hugged her bony figure, brushing a light kiss over the governess's cheek. "How good it is to see you!"

A door slammed below them and a male voice called, "Skeggs, you rogue, where the devil are you?"

Favia's tawny eyebrows went up, and Miss Vennor explained in a low voice, "A visitor for the young ruffian my landlady has taken in hand. It was that gentleman who brought the boy here, and a sorrier sight you've never seen. The poor wretch had been beaten by his master, a peddler of some sort."

Heavens! though Favia. Another of those charitable souls like Mama who commit others to the responsibility of their good deeds.

Nevertheless, she peered over the balustrade and saw that straight back of a man in fashionable gray pantaloons and a well-fitted blue coat that would have done credit to the Regent's set. He wore no hat, and the stream of light from Miss Vennor's room gleamed on ruddy, bronze hair brushed in a short, simple fashion that seemed extraordinary by comparison with the elaborate Corinthian coiffures achieved by the aristocrats of her acquaintances; yet, even from the back, this tall, excellently built man looked familiar.

"Who is he?" she whispered.

"You won't credit it, my dear, but he is the Member with that Sussex constituency, the one who is forever speaking in Commons against His Royal Highness."

"Not Stephen Spencer Kyle! I can't escape the man." She leaned further over the dusty railing to get a better look at him, but he had apparently seen his friend, the peddler's boy, and strode down the hall, out of her sight.

Miss Vennor drew her along the upper hall, away from the stairs.

"I confess, I felt as you do, but he seems to be sincere. He has done much good among the—" She glanced around at the dark, time-stained surroundings. "That is to say, among the poor."

"I know his sort, to my sorrow." If he really was like

12

her mother in his superficial charity, she wondered who cared for his charity objects, once he gave them over to others?

Nevertheless, she was aware of a quickened heartbeat. The realization made her cross, but the sight of her governess, watching her intently, almost anxiously, reminded her of more important matters.

The devil take the man! He was most unlikely to recognize her tonight, even if she were not in masquerade. She set her mouth and determined, not for the first time, to forget him.

CHAPTER TWO

In Miss Vennor's own neat, spotlessly clean room with its few but excellent pieces of heavy Jacobean furniture, the governess closed the door and received the nosegay of violets and rosebuds Favia had brought her.

Nothing was said about the package of books Favia set on the old, inlaid blanket chest beside the bed. The books might carry a hint of charity, and Minta Vennor was proud. Both she and Favia were aware that a small, unobtrusive bag containing twenty guineas had been laid down between two morocco-bound volumes. As though by mutual consent, both women knew that if no attention was called to the money, it might change hands without being considered charity.

Miss Vennor said, "Now we may be pleasant and undisturbed here. I do so enjoy the view of His Highness's Pavilion from my window. Such a handsome young man! He is a fairy-tale prince to many women, but none would know better than you about that, Lady Favia."

Favia had a sudden flashing memory of His Royal Highness, the Prince Regent, as she had seen him recently in London at Carlton House, so stout he must go corseted, his manner charming to acquaintances, indifferent to the

14

point of rudeness toward those closest to him. His Highness had traveled far from the handsome fairy-tale prince of his youth. Still, Favia herself enjoyed association with him, so long as she could avoid becoming one in his long line of mistresses.

Favia went to the long window and looked out over the rooftops to the famed Pavilion, that remarkable series of onion domes sparkling in the afternoon light, a monument either to the Regent's bad taste or his exuberance, or both. An enormous erection in so small a city, but then, that, too, would appeal to the Prince, just as he himself was the sun and center of his coterie. The interior was a series of wonders, exactly suited to the Masquerade Ball tonight, since it never looked quite real. The Brighton Pavilion, with its several wondrous "eastern" salons, was an oriental edifice that masqueraded as the palace of a Hanoverian prince.

"I find the sea both soothing and bracing," Miss Vennor remarked, joining Favia at the window. "It lends variety to my life."

Favia touched her hand, whose misshapen fingers curled into her palms. "I wish we could give your life more—variety."

Miss Vennor sniffed. "I assure you, I have quite enough of that in my life. One never knows what strange creature will next set foot in this house." She studied Favia in a worried way. "My dear child, do things go well with you? That gown looks a bit—just a trifle—"

Favia laughed. "Last time I visited you, I was accosted by half a dozen beggars. This time, I may very well be accepted in some local beggars' guild."

"I trust it won't come to that. Tell me your plans. What do you wear to the masquerade tonight? I've heard of it, you see."

15

They spent the next hour discussing Favia's plans, invitations, and wardrobe for the Season, but between these trivial subjects Favia tried to elicit advice for her conduct, even for her future, without precisely requesting it. Miss Vennor had always been sensible and far more helpful than the Countess of Dalreagh.

When Favia left her old friend and mentor, she felt that Minta Vennor's spirits seemed to have improved. A selfish hope, because Favia was all too aware that it was based on dreams, Miss Vennor's effort to live Favia's fashionable life in her imagination.

Clinging to that optimism about her friend, Favia went down the stairs. In the half light of the entry hall below, a long-legged, sharp-eyed youth about sixteen or so held onto the newel post and swung back and forth. He stopped swinging and his eyes narrowed as he watched her. She noticed that his legs below the grease-stained breeches bore long-healed scars. Was he Stephen Kyle's rescued "wretch"?

Favia looked over the stair rail, wondering if Kyle was nearby. What would his reaction be at this meeting? Despite her firm intention to ignore the man who had ignored her when she was at a vulnerable age, the question intrigued her. She moved down the stairs, trying not to show the slightest nervousness, but she was forced to admit that the youth's insolent black eyes promised trouble.

He moved from the newel post to bar her way, stretching one scrawny arm to the stair wall. When she reached him, she said coolly, "Your pardon," and attempted to pass him.

"Where's Yer Highness off to so quick-like?" he wanted to know. He remained there, barricading her on the bottom stair.

16

Anger welled up inside her, but luckily she retained her confident, amused facade.

"I'm off to meet His Majesty, of course. The king and I are drinking tea. Shall we see you there?"

As the luckless King George the Third was popularly reputed to be mad and under restraints, the boy rightly took this as her peculiar humor. He gave her a crooked grin, but did not give way.

"Sure now, I got no ticket to join 'im. Y'er a mighty pretty thing. Wha'd be said if'n I kissed ye?"

"I should think one of those females behind you would have something to say—with a broom handle."

When he turned, obviously startled, she swept past him quickly, but before she reached the door he discovered her ruse and yanked at her reticule.

"I'd ought to have some'ut for me trouble."

She pulled back, considerably testing the strength of the slender cords that closed the silk bag. He slouched forward, tugging harder. She saw his grin, but was in no mood for this half-teasing attempt at theft.

She muttered, "How dare you, you—you impossible child!"

While they tugged ridiculously back and forth, they were both surprised by a crisp voice of command.

"Skeggs, what the devil are you about?"

Stephen Spencer Kyle slapped the newel post so hard both his listeners jumped.

"Give the young woman her purse, damn you!"

Lady Favia Dalreagh could not remember a time in her life when she had been "the young woman" to anyone. It had sometimes troubled her that her identity and lineage were so well-known she could never guess anyone's real opinion of her. Now the man who had made a career of

17

insulting His Royal Highness was treating her in very much the same way.

Skeggs had relinquished her reticule, and she decided to forgive the young rogue; he looked so uneasy, and understandably, so rebellious.

"He meant no harm. He said he wanted to kiss me."

Stephen Kyle looked her up and down. "A laudable ambition. Quite inspired, at his age." He seemed amused. At least, his hazel eyes held a glint of humor. She was annoyed at her own susceptibility. His mouth was firmly set, but she found herself wondering as she had eight years ago, what it would be like to be kissed by those lips. There was a curve to them that suggested tenderness and warmth. Perhaps passion as well.

She blinked and avoided his mouth, saying, "You flatter me." She added after an instant, "Sir."

The youthful Skeggs started to slink around behind Kyle, headed along the lower hall. Kyle half turned, perhaps intending to lecture upon the evils of purse-snatching. Favia, seeing that his attention was distracted, opened the door and escaped into the late-afternoon sunlight, which had a sudden chilly edge as a breeze swept in off the sea.

A minute later, very much to her surprise, she heard Stephen Kyle's decisive footsteps behind her. For a glorious instant she thought he had remembered her and was happy to see her. That notion was quickly discarded. He called to her.

"Young woman!"

She looked at him over her shoulder. He walked beside her, but apparently his sole purpose was to defend his foolish, and perhaps criminal, protégé. "The boy is annoying, perhaps, but he will not trouble you again."

"I daresay one of my kisses might have been worth very

18

little. But my reticule contains . . ." She hesitated. He seemed to expend all his sympathy and interest upon the poor, the wretched; so she went on, ". . . all my earthly goods."

She wanted to laugh when he behaved so exactly as she had mentally predicted. He bit his lip, as if regretting his earlier manner, and his supercilious tone softened.

"I'm sorry. Of course, I should have realized. Do you live in Brighton? That is, are you employed here?"

"No," she said honestly, gazing up at him, her great eyes soulful. "I've been turned off without a reference. It was a matter of . . . of kisses again. The young gentleman would have me behave in a manner— But the less said of that, the better. I'd hoped Miss Vennor might know someone. She used to be a governess, employed by the Earl and Countess of Dalreagh, of the haut ton, you know."

"So they believe."

She couldn't mistake the crisp, hard feeling in that remark. Was he a revolutionary? She had never thought he would go so far, but he would not be the first Englishman of solid background who let himself be captivated by the bright promise of the American and French revolutions. She snapped, "You talk like a Jacobin!" but she wondered how far he would go in his radical notions. He might be even more dangerous than His Highness and his advisers believed. She asked innocently, "Sir, do you really believe the Royal Family and all aristocrats should be guillotined?"

He was in the process of boosting her over a gutter running with filth. Enjoying his touch, she was also grateful for his hand. She felt guilty over her attempt to trick him into a confession of treason. She needn't have concerned herself. He merely laughed and teased away her accusation.

"No, my dear girl. I am not a Robespierre. Nor do I have a Danton's skill with words."

"Surely, your eloquence makes you a Danton of sorts."

"Not I. You haven't told me. Have you lost your employment entirely? Tell me. I may be able to help you. Or do you continue to count upon your noble friends, these Dalreaghs and their sort?" His hand was firm and warm under her elbow. The sensation excited her, but his attitude about her family was offensive and quite inaccurate. Her mother was forever taking the first steps in some charitable action, and her father had been notoriously generous.

Pride won out over the pleasure of his touch, and she said, "You need not concern yourself, sir. I have friends. The Dalreaghs are more charitable than you imagine. I shall soon be right and tight again. Make yourself easy on that score."

All the same, she was relieved that he had chosen to walk back toward North Street with her. An unsavory element seemed to have moved into the quaint, older part of the beach town and from the accents she heard as they crossed the crowded streets she suspected most of this element had drifted south from the thieves' kens and slums of London, perhaps in the wake of the Regent and his moneyed friends.

Slipping his arm around her waist, Stephen Kyle lifted her over a peddler's bucket with its pungent seafaring contents and a vicious-looking knife buried to the hilt in a fishhead. The peddler's huge grin showed a gaping hole where several teeth were missing. He called out.

"T'doxy's got mighty fine bones, she 'as. Special about the h'ankle."

Favia gave Stephen Kyle a side-glance and was a trifle surprised to find that he took the peddler's compliment in good part.

"I collect that I am to be flattered by our friend's remarks," she remarked dryly.

He smiled. She discovered that he himself was looking at her with flattering interest, the light in his eyes lively and teasing.

"May I say, the sight of you gives us all pleasure, Miss— Miss . . . ?"

Flustered, she gave the first name that might suit her unexpected role.

"Libbie Beckett, if it please you, sir." She bobbed a little curtsy that she had seen the real Beckett perform. She was pleased by her masquerade. It seemed far more successful with this maddeningly attractive man than her own identity. In fact, she had every reason to believe he would despise her as Lady Favia Dalreagh, the daughter of a peer for whom he had nothing but contempt.

He surprised her again by the curious objection, "It doesn't please me particularly, but I daresay, my opinion of the matter was never solicited."

That made her laugh. She was enjoying herself and certainly would have liked to continue the masquerade. Favia's good sense, however, warned her that this fascinating but not unobservant man would very soon trap her into revealing herself. She looked around, saw that they had reached the shop of the only fashionable milliner in Brighton who did not know her.

"Your pardon, sir, but I must leave you now. I am in hopes of taking a post with Madame d'Arbolete. As a seamstress." Surely milliners did employ seamstresses!

"Excellent. I wish you luck. Shall I venture into the place and speak for you? Tell them that from my experiences you are an adept?"

She assured him demurely that he need not do so. "They might ask embarrassing questions about how you learned of my talents."

"Very true. So then, we make our farewells?" He reached for her. It looked very much as though he might pinch her chin.

"I fear so," she said quickly. "I am very grateful, sir." She curtsied again, respectfully, and hurried into the shop before any of her acquaintances could see the fellow treating her in this familiar fashion.

From the center of the dainty shop with its collection of ladies' cloth heads adorned by various shallow poke bonnets, she peered back out through one of the two bow windows. She watched Stephen Kyle's tall figure as he strolled across North Street looking odd but no less attractive in his hatless condition, his light bronze hair catching the sunset light.

"Mees, you wish to view our confections?"

A small figure in black, buxom but not stout, stood behind her, cold-eyed as no vendeuse had ever been with Lady Favia Dalreagh. The realization startled Favia. For a brief few seconds she felt as though she really had become Libbie Beckett. She was humiliated by the woman's eyes and her contempt directed at a young woman, a "doxy," as the fish peddler had called Favia. She hesitated, unsure whether to disclose her true identity. But her natural combativeness came to the fore, and she decided to play out her role. She became shy, nervous.

"Nay, mum, I come in to miss a gent what 'as 'is h'eyes on me person."

Madame d'Arbolete drew herself up, her bosom expanding with indigation. "*Eh, bien!* Out, if you please, We have no time for little child games."

Remembering her role, Favia let herself be chased out to the street, but her fading green bonnet concealed a set jaw and a smile that would have warned her friends.

CHAPTER THREE

Trying not to reveal impatience, Favia listened to eager Miss Durrance's fulsome praise and her mother's none-too-subtle hints while Libbie Beckett took the black satin mask from Favia's fingers and set it tentatively against her face.

"Oh, mum, just you hide the sparkle in them eyes, or there's no mistakin' who you are."

Miss Durrance put in at once, "Not but what anyone of breeding would recognize Your Ladyship's manner at once. So affable."

"True enough, my dear," the countess agreed. "Do try for a trifle more reserve. I am persuaded His Highness will find you irresistible."

Favia wrinkled her nose at her own reflection.

"Thank you, Mama. Miss Durrance. You are both such comforts."

Miss Durrance's plump face lighted with pleasure, but Beckett giggled, then covered her mouth and pretended she had not heard the exchange about His Highness.

What does she really think of me? Favia wondered. Until today she had seldom if ever worried about the thoughts of servants, or their opinions. She had been reared to treat them well, but they remained out of her ken, her understanding of them being vague.

It had been a new experience, pretending to be her own maid, and she found it discomfiting. All her notions of man's (or woman's) place in the universe were overset by her accidental masquerade as Libbie Beckett. Heretofore, her knowledge of such playacting was confined to the theater with *She Stoops to Conquer* and similar masquerades.

There was no gainsaying that it had succeeded remarkably well with playwright Goldsmith's hero, Would it work as well in bringing a radical Member of Parliament to heel?

Meanwhile, she was faced by an interesting dilemma. Since both Lady Favia and Stephen Kyle had received invitations, virtually commands, to attend the masquerade at Prinny's Pavilion, it seemed likely that her smaller masquerade as "Libbie Beckett" would be exposed. She was surprised by her reluctance to surrender the role of an unfortunate, unemployed object of Kyle's interest and compassion.

He had no very high opinion of the unknown Favia Dalreagh. He would certainly despise Favia when he learned the truth. Her real concern, she admitted to herself, was the loss of Mr. Stephen Kyle's interest.

The countess watched critically as Favia considered her face, masked and unmasked.

"You will never be recognized. You must take care to let His Highness know who you are in some subtle way, or all our efforts are in vain."

"Efforts, Mother? Whatever your efforts, mine are very little concerned with Prinny."

The countess was bewildered. "But you know very well we must have the Regent's goodwill if we are to—" She glanced at the eager, listening Beckett. "Run along, child.

25

And Durrance, enjoy the evening. Lady Favia will do very well now.''

Miss Durrance, being thanked again, departed with all the appurtenances usually needed to occupy the countess. Books, needlework, and the latest issue of *La Belle Assemblée* went with her. Favia looked after the reluctant, retreating Beckett and remembered what it had been like to be treated with so little concern for her feelings.

"Thank you, Libbie. You were of great help.''

The girl gave her one of her quick smiles, almost a smirk, flashing on and off, before she left Favia's cheerful white and gold bedchamber. Favia was sure she lingered near the door, but the doors were of oak, and unless they remained ajar, it would be impossible to hear any conversation through them.

"Now, Mother, we must have an understanding. I do not propose to succeed Lady Bessborough as the Regent's mistress.''

Her mother, who looked fragile and lovely in a Roman matron's gently flowing gown, gave serious consideration to Favia as King Arthur's fair Guinevere.

Favia frowned. She was uncomfortable with the polished metal circlet across her forehead. It blazed over her wheat-gold wig, the exact shade of her own hair. The wig was braided in the legendary fashion, so that she looked quite unlike the young woman Stephen Kyle had found intriguing. That masquerader had worn her hair piled high and curly, concealed by her bonnet, except for the breeze-blown curls that crept out around her face. Her blue eyes had looked innocent and inquiring in the disguise of "Libbie Beckett.'' Now, in her queenly gown of blue-and-gold silk and damask, her eyes gazed ahead, proud and direct. Her generous mouth with its full lips seemed more severe, to her observation.

Perhaps, with the upper half of her face concealed by a vizard, that helpful black mask, he would not guess her identity. That would be at once tantalizing and maddening. Would he ever become interested in Favia Dalreagh as herself?

"If he is to do so, it must depend upon my own ability. Or my wiles," she said wryly.

The countess was understandably confused by this comment.

"What on earth do you mean?"

Favia evaded the matter hurriedly.

Hibbings, the wizened coachman hired to replace the bluff, familiar coachman now in the employ of the new Earl of Dalreagh, arrived to announce that the aging Dalreagh coach was ready for its journey.

Favia knew the present journey from the rented Dalreagh house to the Royal Pavilion could be made on foot in a matter of minutes, but it was not her mother's way of travel, and such athletic democracy would have shocked the Prince Regent's circle; so she followed the countess into the coach with the punctilious aid of two Dalreagh footmen. Favia had recently set these underemployed young men to work as postilions, which they preferred, their red and gold livery being much admired by all the pretty abigails and housemaids in Brighton.

The Dalreagh coach rattled through a grassy park interspersed with carefully pruned trees and pulled up to dispatch the two ladies just as a dashing new calèche and a two-horse team rolled around the east flank of the long Oriental series of towers and cleverly maneuvered into place ahead of the Dalreaghs under the guest dome of the Pavilion.

The countess let down the window and peered out.

"That dreadful Hungerford female has managed to cut

in upon us. Such a sad want of conduct as that creature has! One wonders that the Duke of Hungerford found anything in her encroaching ways to make him bestow his title upon her.''

Favia remarked dryly, ''He is dead how, poor man; so we shall never know.''

''She drove him to it, I make no doubt.''

''You must set that to the French account, Mother. Beatrix had nothing to do with the Battle of Waterloo.''

''Perhaps, we should have set Beatrix Hungerford rather than her wretched husband against Bonaparte.''

The made Favia laugh. ''Not against a Frenchman, Mama. I am persuaded most Frenchmen would find her irresistible.''

''Stuff! The woman is singularly unattractive.''

At that moment the door was opened and the steps let down. Good manners forced the countess to change her manner rapidly, since Beatrix Hungerford had waited to enter the celebrated Pavilion with the Dalreagh women.

The duchess was about Favia's height, though several years older, and the two women were perfect foils, having learned long ago that this startling contrast between them attracted much admiration to both. Even His Highness, the Prince Regent, had been heard to remark that there was only one sight more beautiful than either peeress, and that was the sight of them together.

Beatrix Hungerford had the voluptuous, sloe-eyed beauty of her Spanish grandmother, but any touch of Iberian indolence or a habit of siestas was merely a facade in the young duchess, as her enemies and rivals knew too well.

''Above all,'' it was popularly said, ''beware when Bice shows her fine, large teeth in her celebrated smile. She is planning something, and it bodes ill for the person who warms to that smile.''

Shrouded in a cloak of white velvet that made her famous rubies glisten like great drops of blood, she smiled now at the Dalreagh Ladies.

"Countess, how good to see you out of mourning! What a fragile little person you look! And Favia." Her heavy-lidded eyes narrowed slightly. "Spectacular as always, I see. Dear, do you think the Dalreagh sapphires are quite right for you?"

"My own sapphires, my dear Duchess. Not a part of the Dalreagh entailment. But how kind that you noticed," Favia purred as they embraced. "Yes. Fortunately, at my age, one may still be daring. Naturally, I will hesitate when I reach more mature years. But until I am twenty-five, I shan't have to consider such matters."

As the duchess had recently celebrated her twenty-fifth birthday, her smile wavered for an instant before she recovered. Her heart-shaped headdress and glimpses of her black-velvet gown with the breathtaking ruby necklace, earbobs and wristlets, showed her to be a Tudor queen.

"Queen of Scots, madam?" the countess asked, demonstrating a patrician's contempt for the hoi polloi.

Beatrix Hungerford laughed. "I fear I haven't the temperament for her. I am Bloody Mary, of course."

With a deal of light, metallic merriment the ladies were deprived of their wraps and ushered through the long, breathtaking promenade apartments in which they felt themselves, as always, exiles trapped in the palace of a Manchu emperor. The countess kept her eyes firmly fixed on some invisible point just above the lintel of the room through which they passed, and the Duchess Beatrix opened her mirrored fan to flirt with any fortunate males along the sidelines, but the magnificent domed ceilings with their gigantic gold leaf pattern above the hanging chandeliers, one of them dripping diamondlike drops, excited Favia's admiration, as did her favorite objects, the exquisite silken wallpapers depicting the bird and plant life of far-off Cathay.

This promenade gave their many admirers an opportunity to observe the perfect proportions of Favia and Beatrix Hungerford when their wraps had been removed. The Countess of Dalreagh was soon joined by the more mature ladies of Prince's circle, a group with whom His Highness was always comfortable, since the stout, lascivious Regent would remain forever the handsome, young Prince Charming of their youthful dreams.

Meanwhile, those two friendly rivals, Beatrix Hungerford and Favia, arranged each mask over the other's eyes.

"Charming," Beatrix murmured, gliding backward a few steps to gain a true perspective. "So youthful! Like a sweet child masquerading as Mama-Queen."

With all innocence Favia expressed her gratitude for the dubious compliment. "I am persuaded Your Grace is in the right of it. I appreciate the view of a mature female, so wise with experience."

Luckily, Her Grace's humor was equal to the occasion. She laughed, took Favia's arm, and as further doors were opened, they were met in the superb Music Chamber by half a dozen sprigs of nobility in assorted costumes that would have confounded a historian.

Favia and the duchess agreed upon one matter. The duchess opened and waved her fan, not in the age-old language of flirtation but to counter the stifling air.

"Heavens, if only someone would persuade Prinney that a breath of air does no harm! I vow, I would bow to her as Prinney's queen."

A youth scarcely twenty appeared to escort Lady Favia on the excuse that he himself had chosen to be the legendary King Arthur. Since he was a newcomer to the Royal

Pavilion and had already imbibed too much of the Regent's excellent champagne, Favia was relieved when he was seized upon by his formidable mother, who labored under the delusion that Favia was responsible for his somewhat addled condition.

The duchess tapped the sticks of her fan across Favia's shoulder.

"My dear, who would suspect you of leading youth down the garden path? It is too droll."

Favia had to agree that the jest was certainly upon her. She was caught in the middle of the laughing admission by the duchess's hand, the long fingers grasping her wrist quickly.

"He has come. Actually. The Great Man himself. I never thought he would. What insouciance! Or do I mean daring?"

"Who? Not His Highness?"

"What an idea! As though poor old Prinny waddling in would cause all that stir. Listen. I dare swear, everyone is watching him. The man has—what?"

"Insolence?" All the same, Favia watched the entrance of Stephen Spencer Kyle with great interest, which perhaps even exceeded that of her friend.

"No, no. What an air of confidence! That tall, rapierlike form. I do believe Stephen Kyle is the finest figure of a male in this room."

"Not difficult to achieve," Favia noted dryly; but her pulse was beating with annoying rapidity. She raised her fingers, touched the small black-satin vizard that formed oblique frames for her eyes.

Would he recognize her? She was torn by hopes and fears. She didn't want him to recognize his helpless little abigail as a member of the villainous Dalreagh family. But if he discovered that he knew her, this would prove that he did recall her, after all. It would tell her she was not a nonentity, a face and manner and voice he had forgotten, not once, but twice in Favia's life.

The long, exotic room buzzed with gossip, but two men approached Kyle and began a low-voiced conversation. Favia suspected they were discussing his prospective behavior when recognized by His Royal Highness. He seemed amused. Favia saw him smile and shrug as he moved the length of the room surrounded now by several other guests, both male and female, who offered congratulations on his invitation to the Regent's presence or else advice on his conduct when the great confrontation should take place.

"My dear," Beatrix breathed beside her, "what a very attractive man he is, to be sure. Did I tell you, he and I became great friends after an evening at the Revelstokes' Ball? . . . But there. You were not in attendance; were you? What a pity! All the Whigs with any power were there."

"I remember, Bice. I was at Carlton House that night. You know how His Highness feels about the Whigs these days. Even the poor old king could not be more of a Tory, ever since the Prince was made Regent."

The duchess sighed. Her sympathy for the unfortunate King George III, locked into some mental world of his own, was shallow at best.

"I collect that Prinny's Tories cut more of a dash than those tiresome Whigs with their everlasting complaints about the effect of the Corn Laws upon the lower classes, and other boring subjects. But one does meet such attractive creatures, like Mr. Kyle." She patted the tight busk of her gown, straightened, showing her figure to its best advantage, and swept across the room to the huddle of amateur musicians chosen by the Prince Regent for tonight's entertainment.

Favia envied the confidence with which the duchess approached Kyle and two of his friends, standing just beyond a violinist who was plucking strings and listening with an ear to his instrument. Upon the approach of the duchess, Kyle's friends bowed and moved away to other groups. It did not appear to Favia's critical eyes that he was especially pleased to see her. He wore no mask, and was in the evening clothes expected of a gentleman at a dinner party, with that immaculate simplicity the men of better taste had borrowed from the Prince's banished favorite, Mr. Brummell.

Beatrix Hungerford removed her own vizard with a graceful, flirtatious movement, and Favia saw to her own discomfort that Kyle recognized the duchess. She made some remark that caused him to shrug, but seconds later it was obvious she had mentioned something to which he replied with interest. While Favia watched them, ignoring the flattery bestowed upon her by two young men at her side, an usher flung the far doors open abruptly, in the way the Prince Regent preferred, and His Royal Highness bustled in.

Even the elderly ladies furnished with straight-backed chairs arose at once. There was a tremendous creaking of joints, rustling of stiff silks, and snapping of stays, both male and female, as His Royal Highness made his progress around the room in his jovial way, teasing one deeply curtsying lady, punctilious with another grande dame, tossing a light remark here and there to a male crony, until he reached Stephen Spencer Kyle.

Favia caught her breath. Clearly the Regent did not recognize him at once. He acknowledged Kyle's bow with a gracious remark and was already taking the duchess's hand, bringing her to her feet with a deft compliment and his obvious personal interest.

Dressed flamboyantly in the velvet and lace of a Cavalier, he looked stouter than ever, in spite of his corset, but Favia marveled that he retained all of his graciousness and charm. According to his previous mistresses, that manner hardened into complete selfishness and an indifference amounting to cruelty toward those he knew well.

The clever thing, Favia thought, would be to remain the Prince's "flirt" and no more. She smiled at her own naïveté. But Beatrix Hungerford was following this advice, triumphantly.

An aide, close at hand, whispered something in the Regent's ear, and he dropped the duchess's hand, glanced back at Stephen Kyle, and without losing his friendly air, called out, "Ah, yes. Our *radical* friend. We must have a word about these new *radical* politics, later."

It was the first time many present had heard the word in connection with a man accepted by His Highness's circle. The word *radical* seemed to be a new creation, referring to those who were active in trying to repeal the Corn Laws. But precisely what the Corn Laws might be was still a mystery to Favia. Her only connection with them was a remembrance of her father's opinion expressed once in opposition to his Tory friends: "These damnable Corn Laws merely keep the price of wheat so high they starve out every man, woman, and child who lives upon bread."

From that remark Favia supposed the laws had something to do with high tariffs upon the import of wheat and corn. It was an absurdly small matter by which to overturn a political system and perhaps starve a considerable segment of people in order to enrich a handful of great landowners.

Favia noticed that the group around Stephen Kyle had thinned out dramatically. He was now alone. She liked his ease at such a moment and the way his faint smile remained, even while he inclined his head respectfully and murmured something to the Regent, presumably his thanks. Favia hoped, for Kyle's sake, that His Highness read no insult in that faint sign of amusement.

But from the Regent's manner, his warm, friendly attention to each of his guests as he moved on, Favia realized that he did not know he was being insulted. Such an idea probably never occurred to His Royal Highness.

And now, the Regent was before her. Sinking in her best curtsy, but with the mask still framing her eyes, she saw his own protuberant eyes examine first her face and then her bosom. He held her hand a bit longer than protocol required.

"And how could I not recognize Lady Favia? A man should be horsewhipped who would do so." (She hoped Stephen Kyle heard that.)

Favia murmured, "You are too gracious, sir. I cannot tell you how deeply we appreciated our invitation to your lovely Pavilion. I am quite in awe of its designer."

He blushed faintly, more pleased than ever. "You are aware that much of it was my creation?"

She might have carried out the pretense to her own benefit, but some latent honesty almost lost during her entanglement with the Carlton House set made her shake her head regretfully.

"I fear that I was. Your Highness's talents are too well-known. You cannot hope to conceal them."

That pleased him.

"Charmingly put. As in all things, my dear—" He was recalled to these public surroundings by the sudden quiet that had fallen on the huge room. He altered the intimacy of his remark, "—my dear Lady Favia."

He made even this hackneyed compliment sound sin-

35

cere, and in spite of everything she knew about His Royal Highness, she liked him.

"I hope I may always count Your Highness as a friend."

"You may indeed. And your dear mother. Devotion personified." He looked around. "The countess is present tonight, I trust."

Delighted by his graciousness, Favia indicated her mother and had the satisfaction of seeing His Highness choose the Countess of Dalreagh with whom to share the delights of the "small repast" so dear to his epicurean heart. The countess, who never forgot her distant Plantagenet blood, was not overwhelmed by the attentions of a Hanover prince, but she, too, liked the Regent; so she accepted his arm with suitable smiles and the observation that she had always preferred him to his many brothers and was glad his daughter, the Princess Charlotte, presumptive heir to the throne after the Prince, resembled him rather than her mother.

As the Prince Regent's animosity toward his wife was both well-known and reciprocated, the countess's frankness did her no disservice. He preened complacently under the countess's implied criticism of his wife and gave her his attention for fully ten minutes while he filled her plate with *truite au bleu*, a soupçon of a *faisan sauté*, a brioche *au fromage*, various vegetables, and a mountain of sampled souffles involving exotic fruits.

The countess nibbled at the pineapple soufflé and ignored the rest.

Meanwhile Favia became aware that her smooth-speaking, highly sophisticated Wiltshire neighbor, Vincent, Viscount Kinsham, was taking her arm.

"Shall we follow the great man, my lovely Guinevere?"

"Great man?" She looked around, expecting to see Stephen Kyle but realized self-consciously that the viscount was referring to the Prince Regent. Kyle remained across the room, listening without much excitement to the chatter of Beatrix Hungerford.

Whatever the hopes and expectations of the Dalreagh neighbors in Wiltshire, Favia always felt a trifle uneasy in Viscount Kinsham's presence. Gossip had it that he and a few choice spirits of his class indulged in debauchery, unsavory affairs that would even shock the Regent, if he knew. Despite fortunes from two doting grandmothers, Viscount Kinsham was not considered an eligible connection for a young lady in search of a husband. The oblique slant of his eyes and the set of his thin lips often made him seem to sneer, though Favia felt that she gave as good as she got, and in his light-handed way, he was amusing, besides knowing all the *on-dits* of the day.

He saw too much now.

"The hero of the hour seems to be closely involved with Her Grace. Or had you noticed?"

"I hadn't, frankly." She set her champagne glass down upon the tray offered by a young lackey in a vaguely Oriental livery that did not accord with his light, Celtic features.

By coincidence, however, Favia's heavy necklace of unadorned sapphires became entangled in the gold embroidery of her gown just as she and the viscount moved to the long trays heaped with a hundred delicacies. She knew the Duchess Beatrix was immediately behind her. She couldn't mistake that deep, throaty voice, which had been widely acclaimed as sensuous. Doubtless, the gallant Mr. Kyle accompanied her.

Favia waited while the viscount disengaged the necklace, thus causing a delay among the guests behind her. She turned to express her regrets, directed at Beatrix, ignoring her companion.

37

"So clumsy of me, Your Grace."

The duchess lowered her voice, but her smile, full of mischief, was well-known to Favia.

"Not clumsy, my friend. But all for nothing."

Instinctively Favia betrayed herself by looking at the duchess's escort. He was at least seventy-years-old, Sir Francis Wrede, a gentleman of the previous century. Tonight he was elaborately adorned in blue velvet and gold satin with his bagwig carefully powdered and his silk stocking clocked in a style that was all the crack in his young manhood. He had, in fact, been her grandfather's crony.

Pretending to misunderstand the duchess's sly comment, she gave Sir Francis a radiant smile, asked whether he had enjoyed his recent sojourn taking the waters of Bath, and proceeded with her escort. The viscount's eyes had narrowed at all this byplay, but he merely remarked, "It does one's heart good to see your affection for our more antiquated cavaliers."

"Not at all. I pay respect where it is due."

"And you find the dashing radical has earned that respect?"

She leapt to a defense that was heretofore alien to her. "A man who defends the poor and the aged and even illtreated children has earned anyone's respect."

His smile was somewhat crooked. "Shall I remove that little mask, merely to be certain I am here with carefree Lady Favia and not some vinegar-faced bluestocking?"

She broke down, laughed, and asked, "Am I really so dull tonight?"

"Prodigiously."

"And of course, it was my object to please the heartless Viscount Kinsham."

"Just so." He thrust the elegant crested plate under her

38

chin. "Do you favor the *rôti de veau* or the *jambon à la radicale*?"

She wrinkled her nose at him. "You are not amusing, and Mr. Kyle is not a radical, whatever that my be."

The musicians in the Chinese Music Room had struck up a tune, and many of the guests turned to listen. Favia took this opportunity to look around as well, hoping to glimpse the maddeningly elusive Stephen Kyle.

This proved to be no problem. Everyone in the long room heard the sudden and unaccustomed shrillness of the Regent's voice as he pointed a spoon in the face of a calm, faintly frowning Stephen Kyle.

"You forget yourself, sir. We care very deeply for the welfare of the unfortunates."

Whatever Kyle said in reply was lost in the Regent's angry explosion.

"The import and export duties are not my province, sir. And if they were, I should not raise a finger to act. Let the excise men handle all such nonsense. The Corn Laws, as you call them, have served your country well. They have given protection to the finest of our citizenry, the very soul of this realm. . . . You may retire, Mr. Kyle."

This time there was no mistaking Stephen Kyle's smile. He bowed, took several steps backward, turned, and walked out of the room. He may have been aware that every eye was upon him, but he seemed utterly indifferent to their attention.

"Bravo, Mr. Kyle," Favia whispered, and when the viscount looked at her quizzically, she repeated with an air of defiance, "Bravo!"

"Now, if only this radical returned your admiration," he suggested.

She thought of Kyle and that poor, unfortunate "Libbie Beckett." There had been a quality of tenderness in his interest there. They had enjoyed the beginnings of a delightful flirtation.

"He may have scorned me," she admitted to the viscount, "but I doubt very much if he would scorn 'Libbie Beckett.' "

"Libbie Beckett?" the duchess's deep voice cut in unexpectedly. "My dear, say rather, Beatrix Hungerford."

The viscount and Favia gave her their surprised attention. The viscount wanted to know, "Who is this Libbie Beckett, may one ask?"

"Does it matter?" Beatrix waved away his curiosity. "I assure you, Stephen Kyle is excessively devoted to me. I'll wager that none of his Libbie Becketts or even his Favia Dalreaghs could make him forget . . . but I must take care, lest you think me immodest."

Favia's sense of adventure was aroused by that challenge.

"Who knows? I might ask the viscount to register that wager at Tattersall's, but I shan't embarrass you, dear Beatrix. Heavens! The music is deafening. I can't hear a word you say."

Beatrix raised her voice. "You are afraid of a wager. My dear viscount, you are my witness. She fears a contest between us."

The viscount looked from one woman to the other, clearly interested in the idea she had presented. He extended a hand to each.

"Mesdames, should either of you win, I would not be in the least surprised. But I would regard this Kyle as an extraordinarily lucky fellow. I assume you do not intend to carry through any bethrothal to its ultimate conclusion? May I remind you, however, that you would hardly improve your position in the eyes of His Royal Highness by showing an interest in our radical friend?"

Favia and Beatrix Hungerford stared at each other. The tension was broken when Favia laughed. But Beatrix reminded them, "If Prinny knew the object was to cry off the wedding at some suitable hour, he would think it a great jest to play upon his old enemy."

Favia teased, "Still, it does have a certain republican sound. Mrs. Favia Kyle."

"Ha!" the duchess scoffed. "One may become betrothed to a commoner in Parliament and still remain a peeress. And I could win. I'm certain of it."

"Unlikely, I think."

"But you fear to lay the blunt upon the chance that you will succeed."

Favia bristled. She was also piqued by Stephen Kyle's indifference to her at the Pavilion tonight. "Name the terms, if you've a fancy to lose."

"My dear, what confidence you have in your beauty! I should like to prick that confidence—let us say, to the sum of a thousand guineas?"

"One or fifty. The result would be the same." She was bored with the subject, but pride kept her from retreating.

"Bravo!" The viscount clapped his hands. "And shall I register this wager?"

Favia laughed, dismissing the jest. "How like you, Vincent!"

Here he was, talking nonsense about wagers when she was far more interested in pursuing a light flirtation with Stephen Kyle in her role as the "unfortunate Libbie Beckett."

CHAPTER FOUR

"I shall confess the truth to him. It is the only sporting thing to do," Favia assured herself more than once. Just how she would accomplish this awkward transformation was a matter she reserved for a later time.

Meanwhile, she found it surprisingly difficult to learn where Stephen Spencer Kyle was staying in Brighton. Perhaps a straight question would have been simple. Even the Viscount Kinsham could tell her directly. The problem was that she wanted to meet the M.P. accidentally, as though by chance, and it was important that no one should betray her real identity to him until she could do so.

Her confession must come very soon, but surely, one more meeting of Kyle and "Libbie Beckett" would do no harm and might prove to him that his much despised Dalreaghs were human and even warmhearted. Perhaps one more encounter would confirm to him that she was interesting, even intriguing, as herself, whatever her identity.

One more meeting as "Libbie Beckett". . . .

Quite by chance, as she had hoped, her mother furnished the information she desired.

Over her chocolate tray in bed for next morning the Countess of Dalreagh murmured, "It was a fair evening's entertainment, I should say. You made yourself charming to him. Anyone could see how very attached he seems to be. He is an obliging fellow. Not truly regal, of course, but—''

''Mother. Good heavens, when the old king dies, Prinny will be the fourth George. Isn't that regal enough?''

''Nonsense. Mere German upstarts, the entire Hanover clan. But a conciliating fellow, and I am persuaded he can be useful to us.''

Favia said on a note of irony, ''He will be gratified that you think so. He certainly became regal when he scolded Stephen Spencer Kyle. Quite a setdown! One would think His Highness had never in his life heard of reformers. Mama, Prinny has completely forgotten the days when he was bosom-bows with the reformers in the Whig Party.''

''Oh, well . . . Mr. Kyle. What else is one to do with troublesome creatures like that? Forever plotting to send their betters to the guillotine.''

''Mr. Kyle is British, Mother, and this is England.''

The countess sipped chocolate reflectively. ''All the same, I shouldn't put it beyond him. Dear, have Pebmarsh bring me a glass. I do believe all this hurly-burly has given me a migraine. . . . Favia, do not always be carrying out these little details yourself. What do you think I pay Pebmarsh for?''

Nevertheless, she accepted the hand mirror and traced one faint line across her brow with a porcelain-pale finger.

''One does wonder that a hotel as respectable as Brighton House should accept guests of Mr. Kyle's extreme ideas.''

So he was at Brighton House. That would be considerably off the Marine Parade, but one of the city's better coaching houses. Favia often felt that she and her mother would manage their dwindling income a deal better if they

43

did take the public conveyance on their travels, rather than their elaborate equipage, including coachman, postilions, and many of the comforts of Dalreagh Hall, which was no longer theirs.

Since Favia and her family were not habitués of coaching inns, she must contrive a reason for being found at or near Brighton House, should one of her usual acquaintances come upon her by accident. She considered and discarded several excuses, finally admitting that if she continued to wear garments suitable only to a female with few prospects and no defenders, she would do well to avoid any of those ubiquitous friends of Lady Favia.

Her courage did not quite reach the foolhardy stage. She walked out toward Brighton House while the morning was still fresh. In the late afternoon even the Dalreagh name would not save her reputation if she were seen wandering about the streets unescorted.

From the Steyne promenade she walked purposefully toward the famed coaching inn beyond the lanes and alleys, where the London High Road intersected the city. When several strolling males had stared after her in a puzzled way, one elderly gentleman going so far as to frown, she slowed her pace to the usual mincing or gliding steps expected of a young female. Her country style attracted the wrong sort of attention.

She made her way around the coachyard toward the heavy Tudor front of the Brighton House Inn with its entrance through the ancient, ivy-covered porte cochere. Within the yard itself a coach had just digorged its passengers, and Favia tried to mingle with the heavy-laden, disgruntled travelers as they trouped into the Brighton House.

Not quite sure what she should do, now that she had reached her goal, Favia stood irresolute as the coach passengers divided, five males heading toward the taproom while two men with females bespoke bedchambers above-stairs with private parlors.

A discussion ensued, there being only one private parlor unoccupied. Favia turned away but was arrested by the suggestion of the tapster.

"There'll be Mister Spencer Kyle what has a parlor with a south view of His Highness's new toy, the Pavilion. Mayhap, he'll lend you his parlor. He don't use it over-much."

Favia would have given a deal to know where Mr. Kyle was at this moment. The answer came more rapidly than she might have expected. The female, an officious, stout woman, bustled forward.

"Where may we find this gentleman, this Mr. Kyle?"

"Abovestairs, I collect. Hasn't passed this way, and he ordered a pint for breakfast some minutes gone by."

Even Favia, for all her independence, would not have ventured up the stairs to visit Mr. Kyle in his rooms, but she waited breathlessly, hoping he would come down to deal with the travelers. Mentally she reviewed the story with which she hoped to regale him.

The busy landlord, being applied to, sent the tapster's boy up to "bring down the gentleman at his leisure."

At once, Favia became the hopeful, expectant seeker after a post as lady's maid to a female guest of Brighton House. She tried to imitate some of the habits of her own abigail, the true Libbie Beckett, that sidewise look, half-sly and half-shy, the quick on-and-off smile when she did not think her mistress saw her. When she had rehearsed these little traits, it occurred to her that they would hardly attract Stephen Kyle, and she desisted, settling on the edge of a stiff, ladder-back chair in the entry hall where the M.P. could not possibly miss her.

Sounds on the staircase made her look up quickly and

peer around the pillar that separated the entry from the stairs and the public parlor. The traveler and his lady hurried to the foot of the stairs.

"Could you by chance be the Honorable Stephen Spencer Kyle?" the female demanded in her shrill voice.

While Favia craned her neck to see, she was shocked by a familiar voice, smooth and urbane, with a faint note of worldly contempt for his questioner.

"I, my dear woman? Not by the remotest chance."

Vincent, Viscount Kinsham. The last man in the world she wanted to meet here, in what she thought of as her real masquerade.

Favia retreated rapidly behind the pillar, but her movement had drawn the viscount's attention to her. He passed the travelers, ignoring the woman's sniff and her sharply exhaled "Well!"

Favia looked around for a way out. Any door. Any passage. Even that open doorway inviting her to the convivial taproom.

Too late. He was there studying her through his quizzing glass, one eyebrow raised, his smile all too knowing.

"Extraordinary. I was sure it must be you, Lady Favia, but forgive me if I note that your taste in dress has quite failed you. Or is it merely that you have lost your fortune overnight?"

Her laugh was light but forced.

"I had not thought to meet my friends here in a posting house, so I dressed to suit my surroundings."

"Hardly, my dear." He gestured with the quizzing glass. "There is no one so richly dressed as a cit, and indeed, the place is full of them. Probably wearing their fortunes on their backs." He looked her over again. "Which is more than one may say for you. What intriguing game do you play, wearing what must surely be the costume of your

46

kitchen maid? Are you aware that there is a rent in your skirt? Near the hem.''

It must have occurred yesterday when I tried to elude Mr. Kyle's young protégé, Skeggs, she thought to herself. To Kinsham, she retorted impatiently, ''Don't be more nonsensical than you were born to be. I am here on an errand, of course, and I prefer not to be taken for—for myself.''

He tapped the quizzing glass on the back of his hand, thinking over her explanation and glancing back up the stairs. Slowly his puzzled expression lightened.

''I was just mistaken for our radical firebrand, Stephen Kyle. He is staying at Brighton House. But you were aware of that, were you not? You and Her Grace, the serpent Beatrix, spoke of a wager. You said a mysterious creature by the commonplace name of Libbie might win our firebrand's affections, and by—''

''We were amusing ourselves. No more.''

''But the wager was genuine.''

''It was a jest and not more. I don't propose to win Mr. Kyle's regard and then cry off. What a wretched business that would be!''

''Too late, Favia. You will dishonor yourself if you deny the wager now. What is the harm of such a trick? He deserves it. He certainly shows no interest in Lady Favia Dalreagh. It is your task to prove him wrong. And what better way than by appealing to his well-known sympathies for the lower classes? Hence this appalling masquerade, I assume. Just your way of winning the wager.''

''Don't be absurd.'' What a ridiculous moment! Of all people, Viscount Kinsham was the most likely to satisfy his curiosity. He was also a mischief-maker, a gambler, and, as luck would have it, a witness to Beatrix Hungerford's challenge to Favia. Unfortunately Favia had not refused the wager at the moment it was made. Honor and pride (and perhaps her personal desire) were prodding her into the wager.

Meanwhile her silly attempt to play games with Stephen Kyle had ended as it deserved to end, in an absurd failure. The area at the foot of the staircase had become crowded and noisy. Other new arrivals were making their way up the stairs accompanied by a lackey carrying a mound of portmanteaus, valises, and bandboxes. Someone was sure to recognize her soon. She tried to make her way around him.

"If you please, I wish to leave."

He put out one arm to detain her. "Come, my lady. I've never seen your retreat before victory. It isn't like you. Stand to your guns."

"My Lord, must I call the innkeeper?"

He reminded her with sweet reasonableness, "Come now, I do not think you will do so. It would only expose your little masquerade."

Outrageous! She raised her voice. "My Lord! Let me pass."

His soft chuckle grated upon her nerves. For a moment she wondered if she must jostle him to release herself. Then, considering her present masquerade, the worst happened. She saw Stephen Kyle stop behind Vincent Kinsham. His tanned, muscular hand, the hand of a man used to exercise and the out-of-doors, closed around the viscount's forearm. Otherwise he ignored the viscount, who winced painfully.

"Miss Beckett, may I assist you in some way?"

She opened her mouth to speak but was too afraid of the viscount's exposure to answer at once.

"You are quite safe, if you no longer desire this gentleman's attentions."

"Quite safe indeed, Miss—ah—Beckett," the viscount agreed, stepping aside. With his arm free of that viselike grip he rubbed it vigorously. He bowed to her. "I would always lay my blunt upon Libbie Beckett to win." To the cool Mr. Kyle he added, "Servant, sir," and strolled away. He was soon lost in the company of arrival guests being settled in, but Favia had every confidence that he was still watching her. He seemed to take her joking wager with Beatrix seriously. It was a disturbing, if exciting, thought.

"What the devil was he about?" Kyle asked as he escorted her out of the imprisoning little corner toward the entrance doors and the coachyard.

She poured out the story she had prepared.

"Oh, sir, I should never have done so, but I came to this place hoping I might find one of the lady visitors who wished the services of an abigail during her stay in Brighton." She shivered, looking woebegone and pathetic. "But I had no notion—I mean to say—that gentleman treated me like some doxy he could take liberties with." She gazed up at him, her great blue eyes wide with admiration. "It was heroic of you, sir. You saved me."

He laughed at that. "Hardly so far. That fribble isn't likely to prove dangerous in a public place. I suggest, however, that you do not find yourself alone in private with him."

"Indeed not, sir."

They were crossing the pebbled coachyard, and he looked at their surroundings, still amused.

"This is an extraordinary relationship, yours and mine."

She was enjoying this lighthearted teasing too much to end it quite yet with a confession. She asked lightly, "Is it a relationship?"

"A very active one. We have spent every moment of our acquaintance walking about the town. Do you think we

49

might, on the next occasion, remain in one place long enough to learn something about each other?''

"But, sir, I have so little time. I mean to say, I must obtain a post. I made a dreadful mistake in coming here.''

"Not very wise, I grant you. It appears that I must solve your problem, since I so rudely interfered with your efforts to—as you call it—obtain a post.''

"I shouldn't imagine you yourself need an abigail.''

"Not immediately, no.''

"Then, you have a mother?'' Heavens! "Or a wife?''

"Neither. I do have a sister, but she is in Sussex and chooses her own lady's maids.''

"Then, sir, you are not in a position to help me.'' She remembered too late to reduce the impudence in her tone. Luckily he did not appear to notice.

"However, I do have an acquaintance. A lady of quality. Charming. A good employer, I should think. She seems generous, and I make no doubt she will find you eminently suitable.''

"Oh?'' She began to wonder just how she would disentangle herself without prejudicing him forever with her confession. "Perhaps another day. I have one or two calls to make this morning. Possible employers.''

"Rubbish. You are coming with me in my curricle.''

"What nonsense! It would be grossly improper.''

"My tiger is walking my team at the far end of the yard. I am making it my personal mission to find an employer for you. You, on your part, must look your best, and behave with propriety.''

She glanced over at the cherub-faced young rogue who was rubbing down one of a splendid team of bays. The horses seemed a bit fractious. She bristled. "Riding with you, a strange—I mean—a gentleman, what would be said of me?''

"Very well. We will walk."

"Who is this paragon of ladies?"

"Sorry. I thought I had mentioned her. Beautiful creature. The Duchess of Hungerford. Beatrix Hungerford, a widow of recent vintage."

CHAPTER FIVE

Secretly she congratulated herself on her ability to refrain from panic. If her smile wavered, she hoped he would lay this to shyness at the overwhelming opportunity. Beatrix Hungerford's abigail would be even higher in the hierarchy of lady's maids than Lady Favia's personal servants. "Libbie Beckett" might conceivably be awestruck by the prospect.

"What a grand thing that would be!" she cried, clapping her hands, only to clasp one hand over her mouth in dismay. "But it will not do."

"Why not, may I ask?"

"Because—because my very dearest friend, Maria Smith, applied for the post only this morning."

"Still, she may not have succeeded."

"Oh, but Maria is very gifted. I could not hope to excell where Maria—only think. She learned the French way of lacing ribbons through the hair and those sweet little curls on the neck. . . ."

"Here?" His fingers scarcely touched the nape of her neck, under her bonnet. She was shaken by the pleasure of that touch, as no lady should ever be. He had touched her so very lightly, she could pretend she had not noticed, and there would be no need to scold him. She recovered to shrug him off and say in a brisk way, "I believe so. She is far more skilled than I."

"You are too modest. I make no doubt Miss Brown could be put out of countenance by your own light touch."

"No, indeed. She had often been chosen before me."

"I think you will find Her Grace prefers a young woman of your sort. Miss Brown sounds like an officious creature, puffing up her own consequence over a modest person like yourself."

She tried to look demure and was afraid she merely looked guilty. Her conscience trouble her. She tried again. "But today I have several errands. Tomorrow, or even the next day, would be more suitable."

"Perhaps Miss Smith will have failed to please."

"Perhaps."

They were standing much too publicly, near the most popular area of the Marine Parade, when he asked on a casual note, "You have two friends employed by the Duchess of Hungerford?"

"Certainly not." That would be asking too much of coincidence.

"Which of your friends is—I believe you females call it a 'bosom-bow'—Miss Smith or Miss Brown?"

She tried to remember which name she had mentioned first. There was nothing for it but to brazen out her mistake. "Maria Smith, of course. I have no acquaintances named Brown. What a commonplace name! At all events, I cannot go with you today." Hearing herself, she retreated slightly. "I mean to say, I am most grateful, sir. No one could have been more kind. But now, I must—"

"Here, here. Don't rush away. This is not the brave young person I encountered yesterday. Her Grace isn't a woman to admire craven servants."

53

Favia bristled. "I assure you, sir, I am quite the equal of the Duchess of Hungerford in courage." She had been accused of many things in her life but never of cowardice. As though this were not insulting enough, she was being obliquely compared to Beatrix Hungerford. Her Grace would not admire craven servants, indeed! Anyone in her service was liable to be struck by a wildly swinging hand mirror at any moment. Beatrix had even been known to wield a riding crop against her grooms when in a temper.

Stephen Kyle seemed to like her show of spirit. "Excellent. Now you are the girl I remember. Come along." He tucked her hand in his arm, and she found herself hurried across the lane into the Marine Parade and the temporary residence of her old rival, Beatrix Hungerford.

The prospect was not alluring. She could expect no friendly cooperation from that quarter.

Just beyond the Marine Parade and its newer constructions they came to an overpowering, timbered house, pressed between less ornate buildings of recent vintage, purchased by the Duchess of Hungerford with an eye to future profit. In a panic tinged with amusement Flavia let herself be maneuvered around the wrought-iron railing to face a kitchen maid sweeping the front cobbles with a set of broom-straws.

"Good day. Her Grace is at home to visitors?" Kyle asked. His pleasant greeting and his manner were not those he used with the Prince Regent's guests at the masquerade.

The duchess's servant was as impressed as Favia had expected her to be. Her heavy, sullen face bloomed. "Well, then, yez'll find 'er in if y'er a mind to test 'er temper, sor. . . . As ye may well be," she added after a careful study of him.

He thanked her and ushered Favia past her to the heavily brass-and-timber–reinforced front door. Favia barely refrained from warning him that "our Bice never sees callers before noon." She said nothing. She was framing an explanation and pictured herself confessing, "I am not an abigail. Please understand that I did not intend to—" But things moved too quickly.

The imperious Hungerford butler appeared to have been on the watch for Her Grace's friend, Mr. Kyle. He arrived almost on the heels of a servant in the somber black and silver livery of Her Grace's Spanish ancestors. The butler gave Favia a supercilious glance that ended in a frown. She had a strong notion that he was beginning to recall her but was not quite certain she could be the peeress with whose face he was vaguely familiar.

She decided that the only way out of her impasse would be to treat her masquerade as a delightful jest between herself and Beatrix Hungerford. In this way, she could not be said to have made Stephen Kyle a figure of fun. He was merely the innocent party who had made false assumptions when they first met.

Nervously she tried to compose herself and even to prepare a gay and saucy smile, but the smile faded as the Duchess of Hungerford swept into the room in a Spanish morning gown of black silk too heavy for the day's sunny weather. The skirts were even fuller than the new fashion permitted, and she trailed the phenomenal black lengths of a Spanish lace shawl behind her, all of which would have been disastrous to anyone else, but Favia had to admit that on Beatrix the studied black, relieved only by a necklace of pear-shaped diamonds, was not ineffective.

The duchess extended a well-shaped but fleshy hand to Kyle, who brought it nearly to his lips in the gesture she clearly expected. While Favia held her breath, Beatrix shifted her black-eyed gaze from Kyle to his demure companion. She blinked, opened her crimson lips, and her eyebrows went up.

Upon a sudden inspiration Favia bobbed a curtsy and announced more loudly than she had intended, "Libbie Beckett, Your Grace. I'm an abigail by training."

Her Grace's eyebrows lowered. She was quick to understand, but why should she play Favia's game? That was a puzzling question. Since she was an intrigante at heart, perhaps the idea of taking part in this charade interested her.

"Libbie Beckett," she repeated with a thoughtful air. "The name is oddly familiar. Surely, I have heard it before. I wonder. . . . Have you ever been employed by the Dalreaghs? Lady Favia, perhaps?"

"Briefly, ma'am." Favia poured out the words rapidly, wondering why Beatrix had not betrayed her. With reckless daring she added, "A charming lady, but the post was temporary, until her own maid came to her from Wiltshire."

"I recall you were complaining last night," Kyle said. "You said you had been forced to dismiss your own maid for some cause or other. So, I have brought you a young person of accomplishments."

Kyle was looking from one to the other of the two women. Favia thought there appeared to be amusement in his words. At this time, however, Favia was more anxious about Her Grace's reaction.

The duchess's own reply was a bit tart. "I have your word for the doxy's accomplishments, Mr. Kyle. But of course, one cannot rely upon the services required by Lady Favia Dalreagh, her former employer. I am told that the lady is a shrew, a sharp taskmistress, notoriously unwilling to pay her servants." While Favia gasped at these unanswerable insults, the duchess poured further coals of fire on her head.

"And such a dreadful taste in clothing! I would hazard a guess that at this very instant one would be likely to find Lady Favia in some wretched, unfashionable gown, of a color more suitable to a child of fourteen, and looking as demure as makes no matter."

"I had not noticed, ma'am. She seemed very correctly dressed to me," Favia said quickly, trying to keep her tone between respectful and firm. "Naturally, I would try to oblige Your Grace to the best of my ability."

"Upon this hopeful conclusion, I will leave you to work over the details," Kyle announced.

Clearly the duchess had hoped to see more of Mr. Kyle than this brief visit, but he took up her hand before she could offer it and sketched a kiss somewhere above her knuckles without touching the flesh.

Favia was pleased when he reached for her own hand. Though he made no effort to salute it with his lips, in the old-fashioned courtesy gesture, he held it a second or two longer than was customary. His grip remained strong and warm. She rewarded him with a smile in which there was a good deal more freedom than might be expected of a lady's maid. He looked down into her eyes for a long, delicious time. His gaze filled her with excitement.

Then he was gone, and Her Grace, the Duchess Beatrix, seated herself on a stiff, upholstered settee and made room for Favia. It was not a comfortable room, with its crimson portieres so oppressive on these warm spring days, and its exceedingly heavy Spanish furniture, all the shiny black surfaces covered with dust. It seemed to Favia a mirror of its mistress, this crowded, overperfumed room.

"Well, My Lady," the duchess began, "tell me at once,

I am quivering to know. Do you hope to win our little wager by this charade?''

That terrible wager again. Lord Dalreagh had been a sporting man, and Favia was his daughter. She found it impossible to bow out of a wager that was being publicly discussed. There was dishonor either way, and if she lost the wager, worse than dishonor. Sheer financial ruin.

The duchess went on. ''I shouldn't think your masquerade will serve. I mean to say, you don't appear at your best like this, do you?''

Favia reminded her, ''It seems to have served with Mr. Kyle.''

''Bah! All the greater your fall when he discovers your true identity. Shall I ring for some refreshments? My ancestors had a pleasant custom in Spain. Sherry and biscuits. You English have copied it, I note. But, I daresay, your previous employer, Lady Favia, must have told you that.''

Favia refused the sherry with thanks but looked directly at her rival and asked, ''Why didn't you expose me? I expected you to do so.''

The duchess fingered each of the three thickly jeweled rings on her right hand.

''My dear, it is always unwise to divulge one's secrets. However, I will favor you''—she patted Favia's hand—''because we are such old, old friends. You say you expected me to behave thus and so. But I make it a firm rule never to behave as expected. Eventually, I find this serves me well. In your case, who knows where it may end? I am persuaded that in some way, at some time, I shall be rewarded for my silence today.''

It was a disquieting thought. Favia arose. Her smile this time was less genuine, edged with sarcasm. ''I shouldn't be at all surprised. If you will forgive me, I have been absent from home too long. Good day, Your Grace, and many thanks."

The duchess got up also, draping the lacy, flowing shawl around her lower arms. "I understand, My Lady. You will wish to make your great transformation. One can only sympathize with your position when our Member of Parliament discovers your little lie."

Favia wanted nothing so much as to flee from the house, but with an effort she managed to laugh off the duchess's veiled threat and walked out serenely into the busy foot traffic of the Marine Parade.

A sedan chair brought her home to the house on the Steyne in a considerable distress of mind. She was almost relieved when she discovered while changing into a gown more appropriate to her own identity, that the real Libbie Beckett had set about her old tricks again.

"What'll Your La'ship be wearing for callers and the like?" Beckett wanted know. She had already gotten the blue silk out of the clothespress again.

Favia shook her head. "Not that one. The green *gros de Naples*, I think."

Beckett fumbled with the blue barred silk. "Oh, but ma'am, this is more becoming. Ever so. Bring out your eyes, as you might say."

"Not this time. The *gros de Naples*. There. Behind the jonquil walking dress with the spencer."

Beckett must be deliberately obtuse. She drew a gray-green spotted muslin round gown out of the clothespress and held it up.

"Ay. If Your La'ship will excuse the liberty, this makes you look good enough to eat."

"That my be, though I take leave to doubt it." Favia had begun to lose patience. She reached over Beckett's head, took out the Nile-green silk with the new-styled puffs over the upper arms of the long, tight sleeves. "This material is *gros de Naples*."

"But it's not flattering. It's not—"

Favia had worn the gown once before and had received enough compliments to vindicate her own taste. By this time she was convinced that Beckett's motives had nothing to do with Favia's appearance.

The change was managed rapidly, there being a chance of callers arriving at any moment, and when the gown had been fitted smoothly, the curls of her hair carefully arranged in a careless "waterfall," Favia gave her reflection a brief but thoughtful study.

"I'll wear the small matching earbobs."

Out came pearls, then diamonds like teardrops, then her grandmother's rubies that she never wore—

"No, Beckett. The emeralds." These were small and poorly cut, but the color was flattering against her bright hair and matched the *gros de Naples* dress very well.

Beckett fumbled through the ancient jewel chest, peering into the pockets formed by the split taffeta-and-satin–tufted lining, stirring rings and diadems out of their accustomed, individual soft cocoons as if she were kneading bread.

Frowning and laughing at the same time to hide her impatience, Favia reminded her, "Easy does it. We don't want to ruin too many baubles. My heirs are going to suspect the worst of me."

"Could they be caught in one of your new India shawls, ma'am?" the girl ventured. "Seeing as how you drop off your shawls so quick-like."

"Both earrings at once? I think not." With a sigh Favia sat back and looked at her. "Beckett, I want them."

"I'm sure I don't know what you mean, Your Ladyship."

"Beckett. . . ."

The girl's innocent face remained motionless for a few seconds. Then she bustled around the room looking into corners, under the edge of the four-poster bed, which, at Favia's wish, lacked curtains and tester. She glanced over her shoulder, shrugged.

"Not here, ma'am."

"Try again."

Beckett heaved a great, anguished groan of a sigh and moved on. She fumbled around the legs of the rosewood commode near the double doors and came up waving both earrings in triumph.

"Here they are, ma'am. They must've fell off when you come into our bedchamber in one of your hurries."

"Very likely." But Favia had little doubt of how the two earrings found themselves together in this spot. Beckett was fairly successful at concealing things in her palm and then miraculously recovering the objects when forced to do so by Favia's relentless pursuit.

With the small, dangling earbobs in place Favia started out the door to assist her mother whenever the usual chatty visitors arrived with all the *on-dits* from London. In the doorway, however, she paused long enough to warn the abigail, "Next time my jewelry is mislaid, I'm afraid you must go, Beckett."

"But it wasn't my fault, ma'am. The pretty little eardrops fell off when—"

"Next time, Beckett."

"But I swear—"

"Do we understand each other?"

The girl mumbled something, but Favia was already on her way along the gallery above the main staircase and the entrance foyer.

She heard voices at the foot of the stairs and stepped quickly back into the upper hall as she recognized the voice

61

of Stephen Kyle. He mounted the stairs following the butler, who was announcing haughtily that: "The Dowager Countess of Dalreagh agrees to see you briefly, sir, but she asked me to reiterate that she will speak to you only on the subject of servant employment. She wishes you to understand that in no circumstances will she permit the discussion of your—advanced views on reform."

"Quite satisfactory. I understand. I merely wanted a trifling information about a young female formerly employed in the service of Her Ladyship's household."

"Very well, sir, if the terms of the interview are strictly adhered to."

"Quite so."

Evidently this noble defender of the lower classes did not believe in her capabilities as an abigail. He must verify her word with her mother, as if she were a liar. She laughed silently at a belated realization. "But of course, I am."

She waited until he had gone into her mother's receiving parlor. When the butler, Crindle, had left them alone, Favia slipped along the gallery to the cream-and-gold–paneled doors, which remained open. Here she listened unabashedly.

The Countess of Dalreagh was remarking in her plaintive voice, "I am given to understand that you do not wish to convert me on the subject of those dreary Corn Laws."

"Nothing of the sort, ma'am. I merely inquire about a young woman formerly in your employ."

"Indeed, Mr. Kyle." Favia thought with some amusement that her mother had been insulted at the idea of personally hiring her servants. "I am unfamiliar with such matters. Between my butler and my daughter, as well as our man of business in Bristol, they manage these matters.

"An abigail, as I believe they are called. She tells me she was briefly in the Dalreagh employ. I would like to know, if I may, what was Miss Beckett's fault that she was dismissed."

Favia groaned.

The countess was perplexed. "Beckett? Has she been dismissed? I had no notion. I collect that the girl has been light-fingered again. Favia—that is to say, my daughter—is forever complaining about the girl."

"Really? I suspected as much. The girl is startlingly beautiful. Perhaps the Lady Favia is intimidated by that beauty."

The eavesdropping Favia was briefly indignant, then stifled a laugh with her palm over her mouth.

The countess was understandably perplexed. "I should never have described the girl so. Beckett is scarcely more than pretty. She has a certain talent as an abigail. But Favia tells me that this Beckett does actually steal. You understand?"

An anxious little voice whispered in Favia's ear, "Did they mention me? Oh, ma'am, I'm not being turned off, and with a bad character?"

Maddening, to have the real Libbie Beckett hear something of Favia's masquerade. Favia shook her head and motioned her away, but the girl refused to understand, or at all events, she pretended not to understand. "It's about me, ma'am. They're talking of me."

"Nonsense. He wants an abigail for his sister. That is all. Do go, Beckett." She thought rapidly. "I broke the sticks on my new silk fan, the one with the delicate Oriental scene on it. See if you can purchase a similar fan in town."

"Oh, but—"

"Can you do this for me?"

Beckett stared, lowered her gaze, and murmured, "As you say, ma'am."

After this interminable minute or two, the girl retreated upstairs to her own quarters to get her bonnet and shawl.

Meanwhile, to her keen disappointment, the conversation between her mother and Stephen Kyle ended, and Favia heard his booted feet upon the polished, bare floor as he approached the door.

Favia made a scrambling retreat even more rapid than Beckett's departure. She devoutly hoped the real Libbie Beckett hadn't heard any of the conversation between the countess and Stephen Kyle, but she suspected that the girl had understood enough to make trouble for Favia before the matter could be untangled with Stephen Kyle.

As for Mr. Kyle, it seemed a pity his interest in the masquerading "Libbie Beckett" was greater than his interest in the real Favia. His humanitarian tendencies were too strong. It made an explanation much too difficult. Any other male, one like Viscount Kinsham, for instance, would find the whole thing laughable, but Stephen Kyle was not that sort.

CHAPTER SIX

All the forebodings suffered by the Countess of Dalreagh, so soon to become the "Dowager Countess," could not prevent the Dalreagh wedding from being celebrated upon the selected date in June. Despite a knowledge she had possessed for seven months, the countess made the anticipated objections when Favia mentioned the coming journey.

"Dear child, I cannot stir from this house before Sunday. You know how I suffer from the migraine. It came over me this very morning—this hour—and it never leaves until my poor head—"

Miss Durrance, who had been discussing with her the new fuller-skirted fashions and the growing puff of the sleeve, echoed passionately, "Indeed, Lady Favia, Her Ladyship should not be removed at this juncture from her solitude in Brighton. It would be too severe."

"Her solitude in Brighton," Favia reminded them, "is constantly interrupted by invitations from His Highness. Mama, your migraine was far away until I mentioned the journey tomorrow. You must have recalled. I tried to prepare you more than a week ago. I mentioned it after church last Sunday."

With an artistic but genteel moan that made Miss Durrance cry out in sympathy, the countess clutched her golden head. "Child, you cannot conceive the humiliation. To see that dreadful, uncouth woman set in my place, the place your father in his dear way called 'my throne room, my sceptered isle.' . . . Never!"

"Shocking. Almost lèse-majesté, in a sense," Miss Durrance put in, but she avoided Favia's indignant glance.

All very well for Papa to say, Favia thought. But where was he now, when he was needed to undo the errors he had perpetuated in his marriage?

"Very well, Mother. You may be in the right of it. I will make the journey without you. There must be excuses I can offer. Perhaps I myself might take your place at the ceremony and the ball, as Lady of Dalreagh."

Miss Durrance nodded wisely, then caught herself as she saw the way the countess stiffened.

But Favia went on with innocent enthusiasm, "You must tell me what I am to do. There will be so many tributes to me, in your name. How must I behave? The little details that you manage with such grace. You will tell me, won't you?"

The countess fingered the small ribbon rosettes sprinkled over her lavender dressing sacque and looked at Miss Durrance's broad face, seeing nothing but sympathy and admiration. She pursed her lips. "It would be difficult, dear. These are graces that come over a lifetime. I wonder if I should make the effort, after all. I owe it to our name."

"But if you are suffering, ma'am, how cruel that you must force yourself to such a journey!" Miss Durrance put in.

"Very true. But there are occasions when one must rise above personal inconvenience."

"Dear ma'am," Miss Durrance murmured sincerely, "it

is so like you to place duty above personal suffering and discomfort.''

The countess sighed. ''One does what one must. Miss Durrance, would you please ring for Pebmarsh. She will have to pack for me. I cannot have that odious, horse-faced young Worthingham person outfacing me in my own house. I will look my best if it kills me.''

''Oh, indeed, Your Ladyship, one certainly trusts not.'' Miss Durrance dutifully reached for the petit-point bellpull while Favia returned to her own room, relieved to have managed this hurdle without tears and vapors on her mother's part.

A stiff breeze had ruffled the waters beyond the Steyne and blown one of the windows open. Favia reached out to close it and recognized two women gossiping on the promenade with a third, the Duchess of Hungerford's trusted personal maid, standing just out of hearing. Beatrix Hungerford was talking to a demure young woman in a dove-gray bonnet and gown, the latter adorned by a lace collar and cuffs. Libbie Beckett.

Favia had little doubt that Beatrix was discovering all she could about Beckett's past. Any knowledge of that sort would undoubtedly be used against Favia. In what way, she had no idea, but she knew Beatrix Hungerford all too well.

The woman was a notorious gamester and had often wagered on absurdities, even upon such nonsense as whether His Highness would address a female on the left rather than the right as he passed the organ in the Pavilion's magnificent Music Room. She had demanded odds of Vincent Kinsham, another inveterate gamester, upon this likelihood.

Was she attempting at this minute to obtain odds from

Favia's own abigail on the wager she had promoted with Favia herself?

Judging by Libbie Beckett's frequent shrugs and shakes of the head, the duchess could not have been very satisfied in that quarter. Favia smiled and closed the window. The sight of the two together, however, brought memories of the wager, and of Stephen Kyle.

What were his plans? It seemed unlikely that he would remain in Brighton. A lady of the court who offended the Regent might hope to be forgiven one day if she properly abased herself, but there was no hope for a man who had caused His Highness to raise his voice publicly in anger.

She would not see him for several weeks, perhaps for months. First there was the Dalreagh wedding. Then— But the Worthinghams were old admirers of Stephen Kyle and his political views. It was quite possible that he would be a guest at the wedding.

"And I must tell him the truth," she reminded herself. "But in my own way. And perhaps we may start again when he sees that I am not an aristocratic oppressor of abigails who should be on her way to the guillotine!"

The Dalreagh wedding began to loom far more enjoyably on her horizon.

When Libbie Beckett came in some minutes later, Favia expected nothing from her but bland, easy lies and was somewhat surprised when the girl brought up the subject of the duchess while removing her bonnet and apologizing for her failure to get down Lady Favia's travel trunks.

"Oh, my Lady, you've gone and got down those trunks yourself. I'm that sorry! It was all the fault of that duchess lady. Questions. Questions."

"My dear girl, if I needed help, I would have called for someone. I was born in the country. A trifling exercise never hurt anyone. What did Her Grace ask you?"

"I've no notion what she was about, ma'am." The girl whirled around, trying to find an unobtrusive place for her bonnet.

Favia said impatiently, "Just put it down, Beckett. Now, where are my stockings? Set them aside with the shifts for the portmanteau. And those shawls. Let me see . . ." She raised her head. "But what questions did she ask?"

"Nasty, she was. Wanted to know about me and the old days. Like as if I'd done some crime, and that."

Obviously Beatrix was not interested in bringing to justice an unobtrusive lady's maid. But how satisfying if she could bring disgrace and scandal to her chief rival in the Regent's court! Not that scandal was unknown to the haut ton, but it was generally confined to such superior excitement as adultery, murder, and aristocratic debauchery.

"Well, pay her no mind, but I advise you to say nothing if she questions you again. It is quite possible she may investigate your past if you give her any information."

"Oh, ma'am, she'd never! D'you think she'd do such a cruel thing?" Poor Beckett had disclosed her past in that brief howl. Favia could not but pity her.

"Never you mind, for the moment. We'll soon be on our way to Dalreagh. You should be safe for a few days. After that, we will find a way to silence the duchess, if necessary."

"Oh, Your Ladyship!" Beckett's eyes opened wide. She probably thought Favia was contemplating murder.

"I'm sure it will all end very amicably. Now, do be calm."

Libbie Beckett was so overset by Favia's warning that she worked hard to get Favia's travel trunks, portmanteaus, and bandboxes tied up for delivery to the second carriage, without which, the Countess of Dalreagh insisted, she could not be seen upon any high road, even for a period of a week or so, as in this instance. "I have the title to protect," she explained simply. Favia didn't dare to point out that even the title would not be hers for more than a few days longer.

With the blessings of Miss Durrance, who would remain as chatelaine of the rented Brighton house for the week they were gone, the Dalreaghs set out like a medieval queen and her court on progress, spending two nights on the road north and west, at inns known to be "unexceptionable" and sleeping with their own well-aired sheets. On a bright, breezy morning they passed through Bath, once the hub of the court circle, now far more populated by valetudinarians of both sexes, all headed toward the Royal Baths or to enjoy gossip, music, and coffee in the Pump Room.

By early afternoon the heavy coaches, each with the Dalreagh crest, rolled over the muddy wheel tracks of the estate road and down a pleasant slope to a jolting stop in front of Dalreagh Hall. The countess had already balled her tear-stained, lace-edged linen handkerchief into her palm and now brought it up to her eyes again.

"Memories . . . memories. My dear, I always loved this broad view of the house. The splendid Bath stone walls and the soft red patina of the roofs. And all those chimneys. If only the Dower House were more modern! That tiresome ivy shuts out a deal of light. And the cottage is so small. Twelve rooms. What can one do with twelve rooms?"

"Mother, really! Do try not to offend Cousin Martin. After all is said, you must grant that he is the Earl of Dalreagh."

"If your father were alive, he would have something to say to Martin Dalreagh for giving himself airs as though all this were his."

Favia tried not to smile as she spoke. "if Father were

70

here, Martin would not be the earl. But I must remind you that what you call 'all this' belongs to Martin.''

"Please. Do not put me in mind of it."

Favia gave up the attempt to reason with her. Favia could only hope her abrupt and straightforward cousin would show more than his share of compassion and generosity.

The servants were delighted to see the countess. Tilbury, the stout, well-fed butler, who had first opened the front door to the young countess on the morning of her marriage twenty-four years before, met her very nearly with open arms.

"Your Ladyship! It's been a long two months, ma'am. If I may say so." He bowed gallantly from the waist, softening the countess's mood and cheering her considerably before acknowledging Favia with a smaller bow and the smile of a conspirator who shared Favia's affection for the countess. "Welcome to you also, Lady Favia. His Grace is out in the cider orchard. WE expect him momentarily."

Tilbury led the ladies through the dark little hall that opened into large, sunny drawing rooms on either side. The ladies were followed by lank, proud Pebmarsh carrying the countess's jewel case and by demure little Libbie Beckett with her tight smile.

The countess nudged the big double doors open and looked in at the green and gold music salon as she passed on her way to the staircase. "What a pity! The vases on the mantel have been moved. That exquisite gold-banded clock Her Majesty presented to the earl and me on the occasion of our wedding. You must know, I permitted young Martin to retain it. He had no clocks elegant enough for the room. But it is gone."

Tilbury cleared his throat. "I believe His Grace thought Your Ladyship would be happy to have the clock returned to you, seeing as how Miss Elfreda brought clocks of her own. You will find it in the Dower House, ma'am. Properly exhibited with Your Ladyship's exquisite objets d'art."

Vaguely mollified, the countess warmed him with her smile. Tilbury gallantly offered his hand to aid her in climbing stairs she had traveled with grace and ease anytime these past twenty-four years. Favia watched all the attentions with a smile, but with considerable relief as well.

This relief was rapidly dispelled. The countess had supposed she was being led to a private family sitting room where she would be ensconced in her usual chair to receive the new earl in her languid but regal fashion when he returned from his inspection of the fields. Having spoken in kindly fashion to him, she would then be invited to treat the house as hers for the duration of the wedding festivities. After all was said, the house had been hers for nearly a quarter of a century.

Favia hinted uneasily that their own house awaited them. They should become settled there before darkness fell over the wooded countryside and made the work of establishing themselves more difficult by candlelight.

To this advice the Countess of Dalreagh remained smilingly deaf. With the solicitous attention of her maid, Pebmarsh, who had adored and tyrannized over her since the countess's girlhood, she seated herself in the gilt armchair that made up in regal splendor what it lacked in comfort.

The butler bowed low and left her with her little court while he went to announce the arrival of "the countess." He had scarcely been gone five minutes when a tall, leggy woman with a long, equine face strode into the family parlor and went directly to the countess. Elfreda Worthingham's voice was loud and remarkably assertive. Favia thought she would have made an excellent officer barking commands to the unfortunates press-ganged into naval service.

"Good day, Cousin Hermione," she snapped, taking the countess's limp hand and squeezing it. "You're looking well. Do you mind getting up? I think you are sitting on Pug's favorite muttonbone. He is forever hiding it in that old chair."

The countess arose with uncharacteristic rapidity while Miss Worthingham felt around the stiff, worn brocade of the cushion and triumphantly retrieved the dry, colorless, well-chewed center of Pug's world, the legbone of a lamb.

"There! Luckily you have done no damage to it. Heavens, Hermione! Do not look so distressed. It was no fault of yours. You have made Pug the happiest of creatures. . . . Ah! Cousin Favia. Pretty as ever. It never ceases to astonish me that no man has snatched you up. Martin and I often discuss it. He is quite of my thinking on the matter."

Favia did not pursue that opening. She took Cousin Elfreda's hand, smilingly agreed that she had not been "snatched up" yet, and asked after the health of Cousin Martin and of Elfreda's father, Julius Worthingham, a financial figure in the City, whose jovial exterior masked a shrewd mind and an unexpected sympathy with the more advanced Whig politics.

"Papa is in excellent spirits. He rode off to Brighton yesterday. He plans to return with his friend Stephen Spencer Kyle."

Elfreda looked oddly young and vulnerable as she added, still holding Favia's hand, "I collect that your politics are Tory in the extreme, but I would so like these festivities to go off smoothly. You won't quarrel with Papa or Mr. Kyle, do promise me."

Favia laughed at a private thought. "I can certainly promise that, Cousin. But my temper being what it is, perhaps I should keep out of their way."

73

Elfreda hooted in agreement. "Your difficulty is that you say whatever you choose, m'dear. Out with it, that's your method. Far too direct for a female. You should study to cultivate more amenable ways. That's your trouble with males, Favia."

Libbie Beckett covered her mouth to hide her giggle, and Favia almost rolled her eyes. That she should receive lessons on attracting a male, and from Elfreda, of all people, it was the outside of enough! "Thank you, Elfreda," she managed with an effort. It had never been so difficult to remain polite.

She was about to suggest that the time was getting late when, to her exasperation, Cousin Elfreda said abruptly, "Hadn't you better be on your way, Cousin Hermione? Favia? You must have many things to do, to get settled in that sweet cottage, and I'm afraid we will be busy all evening, decorating the chapel with flowers and greenery, that sort of thing. And the sun should be setting within the hour. I am persuaded that His Grace will visit you this evening, in spite of all his attentions to the chapel. You must not concern yourselves. He is sure to make his visit short. A matter of minutes. You ladies must be exhausted after your delays on the road."

"I agree that we cannot remain here. Come, Mother."

The countess had frozen under Cousin Elfreda's repeated conversational thrusts and had to be gently urged on her way by Favia. "Mother. We have so much to do."

Pebmarsh agreed, but more imperiously. "Ay, Your Ladyship. No time to waste here." Over her shoulder Pebmarsh informed Elfreda Worthingham, "The Countess of Dalreagh will receive guests when she has had her proper rest. The countess is a delicate, fragile lady, miss—ma'am. Her guests arrive when she chooses."

The countess raised her chin and moved across the carpet

74

with its crimson and blue pattern that had faded to a blur of ancient Persian bird-and-flower life. Her entourage escorted her out to the staircase.

Elfreda stood there staring for a few seconds before she laughed hoarsely. "Very true. I'll put His Grace in mind of Cousin Hermione's age and frail health." Then she strode after them, signaling to a hovering young footman.

"His Grace's cousins are leaving. The door, my dear boy, the door. Go along and try and be of some use to the ladies. And then see what has happened to the earl. My father and Mr. Kyle should be arriving at some late hour tonight."

Favia drew a deep breath. She realized that once he heard the truth about her, Favia's relationship with Stephen Kyle would be at an end, and the knowledge sickened her. She would lose his regard. But how to retain it as Favia Dalreagh, who had deceived him so easily and ridiculously?

CHAPTER SEVEN

Although Favia was frequently annoyed by her mother's stubborn refusal to accept the changing world, Favia herself secretly shared many of her feelings. It did not escape her notice that the servants at the Hall had grown shockingly careless. There seemed to be no sense of order, no attempt to refurbish or mend worn articles—draperies, recently scarred Chippendale furniture, torn portieres whose hems needed attention. Even the mere act of dusting seemed to have been forgotten.

But Favia knew that any hint or reminder to Elfreda Worthingham would be resented. Worse: It would be ignored. Elfreda herself had met Favia and the countess while wearing a walking dress with a mud-stained hem, and her shoes had tracked cakes of mud up the main staircase.

However, the entailment of Dalreagh and its title had given the property to Martin, with his chosen bride, for good or evil. It was not their property and there was no turning back.

The countess's coach was carefully maneuvered around the west front of the Hall by the wizened little coachman, Hibbings, with his narrow-eyed gaze that appeared to be forever calculating. He brought the wheels safely along the drying wagon ruts on the lane to the Dower House in its charming, if damp, wooded situation beside a bright little rocky stream where violets grew in hidden clusters.

The countess shook out her sodden handkerchief at sight of the ivy-covered brick house with its peaked roof, and once more dabbed at her eyes.

"So like the witch's house in one of those gruesome fairy tales."

Favia laughed but covered her mother's free hand briefly, trying to comfort her.

"You know you enjoy yourself here. You are going to be made comfortable on your chaise, and have your tea and some of Cook's lovely little patés and cakes, just as if you were at His Highness's Pavilion. At all events, you will find the Dower House in better case than Elfreda's household. Heavens! I never saw so much dust. Of course, she is not its mistress yet, until the ceremony, but one would have thought Martin would see what must be done."

"Indeed, m'lady. A disgrace," Pebmarsh sniffed. "But one knows how it is with bachelors, and I daresay, Miss Elfreda has only just arrived at the Hall. Anything else would have been quite improper."

The countess agreed with surprising strength.

"Quite. Do you suppose Elfreda was here in the Hall last night while her father was off visiting with Mr. Kyle in Brighton. One does wonder . . ."

"Mother, somehow, I doubt if what you are implying ever even occurred to Martin or Elfreda. Their marriage looks to me very like an arranged one, for the sake of his estate and her money." Favia felt the nastiness of her own mind in making the observation, but it had been in her thoughts, and she couldn't help wondering. Elfreda seemed so very horselike. She could hardly have been chosen by

Martin for her charm or appearance. Still, men had strange tastes. . . .

Pebmarsh repeated sternly, "I must say, the Hall appeared an absolute disgrace." She sat opposite the countess and offered her a third clean handkerchief in as many hours. "We'll make everything right and tight for Your Ladyship. Mind, now. No running about to see if all's well. You leave that to Miss Favia. You must rest after your dreadful time with that—that person."

The maidservant's virulent disapproval of Elfreda nearly made Favia sympathize with the future countess.

Household servants reinforced Pebmarsh, Beckett, and Favia in escorting the countess across the little stone threshold under its miniature thatched roof and into the long, comfortable country drawing room. A fire crackled in the big grate at the far end of the room, adding a welcome touch at this hour hard on sunset. The ancient casement windows had been replaced in the last century by more modern windows that made the ground floor lighter. This, in addition to the early Georgian furniture of curved and polished burled walnut, formed what might have been a remote but cheerful retreat for a newly married young couple.

Its quiet atmosphere was less appropriate to a woman like the Countess of Dalreagh, used to being enthroned as the center of her large and obsequious court. She entered now, sighing, murmuring, "It is moments like this when I miss your father, my dear. How his great, vital presence would have helped me now!"

Favia, who was doing her best to enliven her mother's arrival home, ignored this comment. "Pebby, you go up to Mama's sitting room. Arrange her chaise longue. See that a small fire is laid in the grate. I'll have water heated for a hip bath. Then you will be cozy, Mama. Come along. Beckett, you see if Cook has mother's tea tray ready.''

By the time the countess had been settled in reasonable comfort with her tea table beside her and Pebmarsh reading to her from the first volume of a chilling romance called *The Abbey Monk,* Favia collapsed onto the bed in her own chamber and ordered Beckett, ''Do not disturb me for anything less than Bonaparte himself.''

Beckett gave a little shriek. ''The Corsican Ogre?''

''They say he is very generous to his ladies.'' Favia sat back on the heavy quilted silk coverlet, with her weight behind her on her wrists. ''Poor man. I don't imagine there will be many mistresses waiting on St. Helena. Clearly I have lost my chance.''

''My Lady! He was the enemy.''

Favia laughed.

Only minutes later she was disturbed by the new footman, who scratched on the door and called, ''Visitor for the countess, my Lady. His Grace is belowstairs. Says he's come to 'do the civil.' ''

''What now?'' Good heavens! Favia sat up straight, touched her artfully careless coiffure, hoping to give it some semblance of order, and went to the door while brushing down her crumpled silk skirts.

''Never mind. I'll attend to the matter.'' She was terrified for fear Martin would throw the countess into the dismals through some accidental remark, and thus plunge the household into gloom for the rest of the night.

Though much younger than the late earl, her Cousin Martin was, strictly speaking, her father's cousin. During the late earl's lifetime Favia and Cousin Martin had led a somewhat cat-and-dog relationship. They were totally unlike and could never agree on anything. Favia's sophistication, her worldly life among the Regent's circle at Carlton

House in London, shocked and disgusted the country-bred Martin. Very early in life he had made it clear that dalliance among the aristocracy was not a matter for jest. Nor was the mental condition of the Regent's unfortunate father.

Though a strong Whig, in policy, Martin had an old-fashioned country squire's reverence for the man who wore the crown, and no matter how "mad" the king was said to be, George the Third was still Martin's ruler and the Prince Regent merely his unfilial son.

The honesty of Martin's convictions Favia never doubted, but she placed great importance on the conduct of the Earl of Dalreagh, as upon what he owed to his house, his household, and the hundreds of tenants who worked his lands. Of late, since his betrothal to the daughter of the passionately democratic Sir Julius Worthingham, he spent all his time and income on various causes sponsored by Worthingham, causes that seemed to have nothing whatever to do with the welfare of his own workers and improvements to the Dalreagh properties.

It was with these troublesome matters in mind that Favia went out into the dark, narrow hall to greet Martin Dalreagh. She was determined to do her best. It was not her place to provoke him.

She was taken aback to find Sir Julius Worthingham with her cousin Martin in the hall. At first glance the noted Whig reformer might have been Martin's father as, indeed, he would soon occupy that position by his daughter's marriage. Both men were stocky, with the frames of men who had known physical labor in the fields.

But the much older Worthingham's crinkled white hair gave his heavy face a bright, cherubic look, at variance with his reputation as one of London's more brilliant minds. Martin, on the other hand, had the square-jawed, stubborn look of a man whose opinions are seldom changed, for good or ill. To soften this front, which might become implacable with age, the new earl's straight, honest gaze was made more direct by what had come to be known in these parts as the "Dalreagh Blue" eyes.

Tonight Martin made Favia's resolution easy for her. He took her two hands, crushed them between his hard-fleshed palms, and spoke half to her, half to his companion. "Pretty as a May bird, wouldn't you say, Sir Julius? And breaking every heart in London."

Worthingham agreed. "And not only in London, I'll be bound. Your most obedient servant, ma'am."

Favia laughed, and leaning over Martin's hands to kiss his cheek, she wondered that she could ever have been cross with him.

"Welcome to Dower House, Your Grace . . . Sir Julius . . . It's good to be home, among friends."

While Worthingham studied her, making her a trifle uneasy, Martin walked along the hall with her arm in his.

"Thank you, Cousin. I hope you'll always regard our home as yours. I'm sorry the countess didn't have time to order tea for you and the dowager. We like to follow the new customs. The countess—our Elfreda"—with a gesture to include Elfreda's father—"thinks it makes for good feeling among the farm folks."

Favia admitted that he was right. After all, her own mother had made her tea ritual famous throughout this corner of Wiltshire. And like her mother, she could not quite bring herself to refer to Elfreda Worthingham as "the countess" before that lady was well and truly married to the new earl.

Moments later, they were invited by Pebmarsh into the "true" countess's sitting room where, to Favia's great relief, her mother was in a slightly patronizing but gracious mood.

81

She accepted Cousin Martin and even received Sir Julius Worthingham who had sired "that dreadfully common Elfreda creature." Sir Julius understood aristocrats like the countess and at once bowed deeply, raising her hand, brushing it with his heavy lips in an unexpectedly graceful manner.

"My dear countess, what a pleasure it is to be received by Your Ladyship!"

The countess beamed upon him and to Favia's astonishment, waved Worthingham to the straight, ladder-back chair just beyond her chaise and tea table.

Martin was obviously delighted by this warmth between the two. Favia thought Martin was trying to promote a personal relationship between the two. Quite possibly he was. If a marriage should be arranged, the countess would then be busy acting as chatelaine and mistress of Worthingham's big Grosvenor Square London house. She would have no time to sit in Dalreagh Hall like a skeleton at the feast, silently criticizing Martin and his wife.

Martin's "Dalreagh Blue" eyes warmed as he, too, kissed the countess's porcelainlike fingers. The countess murmured, "Dear boy, it has been too long. We missed you. How have you gone on these past months?"

"Hard work, ma'am. As the countess says—"

Favia cleared her throat nervously and cut in. "Mother, I believe Sir Julius arrived with Mr. Stephen Kyle. You recall Mr. Kyle."

The countess smiled on a sweet note of sadness. "I vow, the wedding will be lavishly represented by the Whig Party. But there. I do not mean to speak of politics. Come. Tell us, Martin, what have you been about during the months we were so closely involved with His Highness in London, and more recently, in Brighton? How does your Miss

Worthingham occupy her time since her arrival at Dalreagh Hall?''

But she was smiling at Elfreda's father, and Favia had no doubt her interest was expressed for the benefit of Sir Julius.

While this mature flirtation was proceeding rapidly, Favia ached to know where Stephen Kyle might be. She interrupted again, despite a determination not to call unwanted attention to her passionate interest in the ''radical'' Member of Parliament.

''Pardon, Sir Julius, but you did say you came to Dalreagh with your friend, Mr. Kyle, the Member from Sussex?''

''Quite a famous fellow,'' Martin put in. ''Doing wonders to promote action on those infamous Corn Laws.''

And Sir Julius added, ''Infamous, indeed. Yes, Your Ladyship. He felt that he must not intrude on the Countess Hermione until tomorrow when we are all gathered at the Hall.''

''So kind,'' the countess sighed and shed a charming, wistful look upon the financier. ''I am persuaded it was your idea, Sir Julius.''

That gentleman modestly disclaimed while Martin told Favia in an aside, ''Our deplorable neighbor, the Viscount Kinsham, paid us a visit just as Sir Julius and Stephen Kyle rode up. He seemed bent upon speaking to Kyle. Mentioned your name, by the by.'' He went on, innocent of offense, ''Kyle seemed unimpressed. Are you certain he is acquainted with you? These M.P.'s meet so many of us in their quest for votes.''

Favia agreed tartly. ''I believe you must be right. We met so very long ago. He is better acquainted with my mother. He visited her briefly a few days ago in regard to a young female employed by the family.''

"Indeed. Sounds like a very dedicated fellow."

"So it would appear. If you and Sir Julius will forgive me, I have some wardrobe changes to make. For the ceremony."

Martin patted her shoulder. "Just so. You know, Cousin, you seem far more nervous over the affair than Elfreda. She actually said she would prefer a special license and a swift, private affair in London, but naturally, I reminded her of what we owe to the Dalreagh name. The Earls of Dalreagh do not marry quite every day."

"Indeed not."

She made her excuses to her mother and Worthingham, who scarcely missed her, and hurried out. There seemed to be no escape now. If possible, she must make her peace with Stephen Kyle and undo the damage Vincent Kinsham had undoubtedly done with his malicious gossip.

She stopped in her bedchamber long enough to take her green pelisse from the clothespress and ease her arms into it as she went down the staircase and out the door under the tiny, overhanging thatched roof that protected the front steps. By the first rays of moonlight she made out the brook, which wandered through a grassy mere on the east front of the Dower House. As a child she had often played along the banks of the brook, usually sinking ankle-deep in the mud and grass.

But unlike Elfreda Worthingham, she had not been permitted to track her mud and water stains through the Great House. Tonight she ran lightly past the tempting playground of her youth, and in less than five minutes had reached the westerly corner of Dalreagh Hall, where she saw Vincent Kinsham waiting on the carriageway for his dashing Arab mount while he discussed the affairs of the Dalreaghs with an indifferent Stephen Kyle. It was clear to

Favia that Kyle's interest lay in the big black stallion being led to them by the viscount's groom.

Kyle was abrupt, if not rude. "Do not tell me about the greatness of the Dalreaghs. You will find the new earl is a far more worthy squire. He cares about things beyond—all this."

"Well, old fellow," Kinsham said in a jovial way, "you will allow that the Dalreaghs have lived here since time out of mind. They have done very little to improve the world, but they have done wonders in erecting this monument to themselves. A work of art. That should demonstrate their genius for—for—"

"For building?" Favia snapped, pacing the carriageway toward them. "What do you know of the Dalreaghs and the good they have done, the care they have taken of those in their charge?"

"Ah, but, Miss Beckett, you are prejudiced, "Kinsham remarked, which was almost as surprising as Stephen Kyle's conduct. He moved Kinsham aside and took Favia's hand, holding it in his, while he looked down at her. She found herself speechless as his eyes seemed to reflect the glow of moonlight, and she told herself this glow was for her.

"You are very loyal, Libbie Beckett. You defend them despite their lies about you. But why have you returned to their employ?"

"The Dalreaghs lied about this young person?" the viscount wanted to know. "Astonishing. Miss—ah—Beckett, do tell me, how have they lied about you?"

Kyle explained sharply, as though to be rid of him. "They said she had stolen something. The usual excuse of women who are bored with life and wish a change of face in those who serve them."

Kinsham shrugged. "But what else is one to expect when

85

one considers the wagers they make in public, where even Prinny himself may hold the stakes, as it were?'' While Favia felt her heart stop, Kyle refused to show any interest in this.

The viscount went on, after a side-glance at Favia. "But you are right to refuse an interest in such nonsense. Imagine, two grown females wagering which of them will win a proposal of marriage from a man who has not the slightest interest in either of them. What humiliation! For the male involved, of course. I imagine the ladies have no shame. And the entire court is making wagers on the outcome between Lady Favia and the Duchess of—but no more of that.''

Kyle said indifferently, "Good night, Kinsham.''

The viscount grinned, threw a leg over the saddle of the big black stallion, and said, "I leave you to make your peace with Lady—with the lady.'' After flipping them both an impudent salute, he cantered off, followed by his impassive and incurious groom.

Kyle raised Favia's chin with the knuckle of his forefinger. "Here, here. You've done nothing wrong. The blame lies with the Dalreagh woman and her daughter.'' He reconsidered. "Sorry. Not the countess, I think. When I spoke to her, she knew only what her daughter had told her, that you were a thief. What is the truth? Why in heaven's name did you come back to the Dalreagh service?''

She hesitated, but the viscount had made it impossible to betray herself now without being hopelessly compromised by the truths Kinsham had so untruthfully told. She had not wished to humiliate or shame Stephen Kyle, but who would believe that now? Everyone at court must know about the wager, thanks to busy Vincent Kinsham.

If there was only some way she could prove Favia Dalreagh's worth to Stephen, let him see how compassionate and generous she could be! Yes, and humble, too. But to do that she must perform her penance under his eyes. And that posed a problem. Once he learned her identity, he would never go near her, and all her efforts at reformation would be wasted.

She cleared her throat nervously. "I needed the post. The Duchess of Hungerford and I didn't suit."

He looked into her eyes. "Did you steal from Lady Favia, or is she the liar I suspect she may be?"

Her chin went up sharply, causing his forefinger to fall away from her face. "The Lady Favia is not a liar. Never." She recollected and added, "Except social lies. The sort of thing one does around royalty and to please one's friends."

He was silent a few seconds. "Then, you are a thief."

She moistened her lips. "There was a set of . . . a very small set of earbobs. I—mislaid them."

"Mislaid? Then, the Lady Favia did lie."

"No." She was caught and bound in a silken net of untruths. She who boasted that Favia Dalreagh never lied. She felt desperately close to tears.

He did not show the disappointment she had expected. He seemed almost unsurprised. Perhaps he had deliberately maneuvered her into the confession. "Well, then, we have a part of the truth, at all events. I doubt if you would have 'mislaid' jewelry belonging to someone you respected. My sister has had rare good luck with children and young females guilty of many crimes, and her experience has given me considerable knowledge of the subject."

"Like young Skeggs?" she asked on a note of irony. She had not been overjoyed by her own experience with Skeggs in the entry hall of Miss Vennor's lodgings.

He smiled at the memory. "Skeggs is one of my sister's less successful experiments. We are hoping he may fit into

87

the life of a town employer. Thus far, as you discovered, he has a remarkably advanced eye for beauty."

She colored a little, but in the moonlight this made her appear more attractive to him. He stared at her, ran his fingers over her cheekbones, making her tremble at the touch, and suddenly kissed her, his lips lingering all too briefly on her cheek, then the bridge of her nose. She stiffened with anticipation, which made him suddenly aware of the impropriety of his conduct toward the servant employed by his hosts. Before his lips touched her own he drew back, leaving her shaken by disappointment. His apology maddened her.

"I beg your pardon. I very nearly asked you to take employment in my household at Darking Hill. I share it with my sister, Selina. But I'm afraid, after this little episode, you would do well to suspect my motives."

"Not at all. I—"

He pinched her nose. "You should. You are much too beautiful to be toiling in the household of any normal male. Come. I'll walk with you back to your employers. They live in the Dower House, I believe."

In a panic lest he meet Martin Dalreagh or Sir Julius in her company, she protested, "No. I must go. I prefer to go alone. Truly."

She realized that he had totally misunderstood her panic. He said quietly, "I promise you I won't touch you again. You must have had difficulties with many employers who forced their attentions upon you as I did."

"No, sir. Not forced."

Nevertheless, the damage had been done. He seemed determined to prove to her that she could be safe with him. He touched her only once, when he helped her around a marshy spot that had taken over the path. She sighed in secret as she heard the pleasant gurgle of the pond among the grasses and small, white woodland flowers that looked like stars at night. An ideal romantic scene, with the beech trees making a latticework for the moon overhead.

Just as the Dower House came into view she heard footsteps pounding along the path behind them and turned to look back. The young man she recognized as Stephen Kyle's groom in the Brighton House stableyard came rushing up to them. "Master! I been on your trail all day, and yesterday when it come to that. You're needed at home. One of Miss Selina's footmen, he come riding hard into Brighton."

Stephen Kyle shook the groom. "Is she ill? Tell me. What has happened?"

"Caught 'er heel on the stair just afore the midlanding on the big staircase. Snapped her ankle like a bit of driftwood. That abigail of hers is none too heavy in the top loft. Hadn't no notion what's to be done. It was Old Grindle, that highwayman she's made into a gardener, he took her in charge. And he sent the footman to you, sir, in Brighton."

Kyle slapped one fist into the other palm. "And I was off to see a wedding, just to oblige a politician. We'll ride tonight. I'll borrow the Dalreagh curricle. How likely are the changes?"

"I got new mounts, sir."

"Good. We'll do." He remembered Favia and turned to her. At least the earlier tenderness remained in his eyes as he looked at her. "Libbie, if you are not happy with the Dalreaghs, if Lady Favia and her mother mistreat you, I want you to come to my sister, Miss Selina Kyle. The house is near the top of Darking Hill in Sussex. Remember. Darking Hill is the village. It's a sheer rise above the Channel, and the marshes. Here. Use this for conveyance, at need."

He stuffed some coins into her fingers. One silver piece fell, and she stooped to pick it up before he could do so. There were more than three guineas in her hand. She began to protest, but he merely repeated his instruction.

"I've no doubt Selina will need you; so you must not hesitate to come if you feel you would be happy elsewhere than here." He closed her fingers over the money. His voice was low, but she knew the groom must hear and wonder. "Do not be alarmed. I promise you I will not take advantage of your position there." He laughed shortly. "Selina would see to that."

She nodded, speechless, but he was already leaving her. She watched him stride along the path toward Dalreagh Hall with his groom trying to keep up the pace.

Nothing had turned out as Favia had hoped. Stephen Kyle knew less of her than ever, and it was obvious that nothing could persuade him that Favia Dalreagh wasn't a cruel, selfish aristocrat preying upon the misfortunes of poor little abigails.

She looked down at the coins in her hand. Must she remain Libbie Beckett forever? It seemed very probable.

"And I don't even like the girl!"

CHAPTER EIGHT

Within the hour, according to Elfreda Worthingham's report the next morning, Stephen Kyle had been on the high road to Sussex for half the night. Favia credited her with taking the news remarkably well. Elfreda laughingly boasted, "This demonstrates our good Stephen's concern for humanity, and for family. The dear fellow would never have sacrificed the celebration of our nuptials for anything less important than a concern for Miss Selina!"

Everyone seemed to agree except the countess, who remarked privately to Favia, "How like the man! No sense of what he owes to his sponsors in Parliament. Sir Julius has supported all his strange notions, and this is the result. Abandonment at such a time."

Favia, whose own interests were more selfishly centered, asked why the loss of Worthingham's friend at such a moment should be termed "abandonment." "It is not as though Sir Julius were the groom and Mr. Kyle had agreed to stand up with him."

"You persist in misunderstanding, my dear. Sir Julius will be abandoned by his daughter. He explained to me last evening how Miss Elfreda had acted as hostess to his political friends and at the various balls and routs and dinners so necessary in his position.''

''Curious. I never fancied Elfreda as much of a diplomatist.''

The countess sighed and waved away Pebmarsh, who had brought one of her pale golden curls too far over her left temple. ''That's as may be. I could not but remember how it was with the earl alive. We were forever entertaining. I was said to be the best hostess in the West Country. Do you remember?''

''Indeed, I do, Mother.'' Favia squeezed her shoulders and teased, ''I do believe Sir Julius is hanging out for a bride, a certain great lady, to act as his own hostess.''

''What nonsense you talk, dear! As though I could forget so easily the fidelity I owe to the earl.'' But Favia, catching Pebmarsh's eye and the way the abigail's eyebrows went up, suspected that her mother enjoyed the idea of being pursued by an eminently eligible and attractive widower. It was a disturbing thought if her mother had no genuine interest in the man, but perhaps the countess did feel his charm. Sir Julius Worthingham would bear watching.

Then, because she was reasonably honest about herself, Favia remembered that her own peculiar fixation on Stephen Kyle held endless questions. He was constantly in her thoughts during the ceremony in the old chapel, which smelled of moldy leaves and vegetation despite the many flowers placed strategically around the Gothic interior. Even the early fruits had been brought in from the succession houses to aid in the decoration. The high, narrow, stained-glass windows on the east side opened upon the sluggish pond, and Favia was not surprised when Martin announced to Vincent Kinsham during the short wait for the bride that he was about to have the underbrush in the pond cleared away.

Vincent whispered to Favia, "Romantic soul, thinking of drains and sewage at such a time."

The countess, gallantly escorted by Sir Julius Worthingham, made objections as well, but the financier reminded her in a teasing way, "My dear ma'am, in its present condition it is hardly the kind of place for a lady like yourself. Forgive me if I embark upon personal matters, but I do not like to think of Your Ladyship surrounded by dead foliage and mud."

Thinking of it from this viewpoint while Sir Julius went back to the house for his daughter, the countess murmured to Favia, "There may be something in Cousin Martin's plans. I feel that these old walls should be refurbished."

"They've been washed down, Mother. Everything is reasonably clean."

"Yes, but it seems so unsuitable to—I mean to say, I was used to such different surroundings. Sir Julius saw that at once. He is quite right."

"Mother, you lived here for over twenty years, and you entered the chapel so seldom the vicar began to question your Christianity. So don't talk nonsense."

The countess was shocked enough to raise her voice. "Favia, you forget yourself. I invariably called in the vicar to bring Christian comfort to me."

This brought a grin of sly amusement to the viscount's face. Fortunately any comment Favia might have made to her mother was silenced by the precipitate arrival of Elfreda Worthingham with her shorter, heavier father in tow. The bride wore a cream-colored, barred silk gown of the new full-skirted fashion, frilled around the hem, that gave her an opportunity to proceed along the ill-lighted aisle with her accustomed lengthy stride. At the altar Martin Dalreagh, who was slightly shorter than his bride, looked fully able to assert his rights, conjugal and otherwise. His stocky form bulged slightly in his coat, an ill-fitted silk waistcoat, and his black pantaloons, but there was little doubt that the fleshy bulges were muscular, not fat. With moderate pleasure he watched the approach of his prospective bride.

It wasn't until the brief ceremony had ended and the bride and groom were surrounded by the beaming Reverend MacMurdock, plus Sir Julius, Vincent Kinsham, and the household servants, that the countess heard the dreadful title stolen from her, for the first time.

The Reverend MacMurdock bowed to Elfreda Dalreagh. "And now, may I be the first to address—Her Ladyship, the Countess Elfreda of Dalreagh?"

"Dear me, yes, Your Worship." The new countess tucked her arm in her husband's. "And you, Your Lordship."

Favia joined the festive group, embracing the new countess, wishing her long years of happiness. She was a little taken aback by Elfreda's brusque, if friendly, dismissal of such expressions as unnecessary.

"Oh, I shall be. Have no concern, Cousin. It is merely a matter of applying oneself. There is so much to be done in this imperfect world."

Favia couldn't help reminding her lightly, "So much to be done here on the estate, when it comes to that."

"Too true." Something that Favia guessed must be a rat scampered across the bride's instep and vanished amid the moist stones of the floor. Elfreda stamped her sturdy morocco shoe. "Martin, do let us be away from this dreadful tomb. I vow, I shall have the entire edifice torn down, stone by stone, before I am done."

The Dowager Countess moaned, hearing of this intended desecration. Favia, to whom the careless remark had also been an annoying criticism of sacred Dalreagh, reminded her, "If you are never in the chapel, Mama, how can you miss it?"

"I do not voyage to the moon, but I should be sorry indeed to look up one night and find it had vanished."

"She has you there," the viscount whispered, and Favia had to admit he was right. She was a great deal overset when he told her carelessly, over the champagne toasts in the long drawing room, "my man brought the news of Brighton to me an hour since. It seems the duchess has spread news of your little wager and even Prinny has put up the blunt."

"Ridiculous. I haven't the first notion how much would be wagered between us. We have scarcely discussed it." She added emphatically, "not that I approved the wager in the first place. And now you have made it too late to cry off." After a little pause she asked in a careless voice, "How did His Highness wager? On which of us?"

His thin-lipped smile broadened. "Upon yourself. He began at one hundred guineas. At the last word, when my man left Brighton, it was three thousand. Mark me. Before this little race is ended there will be some pockets to let. The demon duchess offers a wager against you personally to equal the stakes Prinny puts up."

Favia would find difficulty raising even half the sum of three thousand guineas unless she risked jewels that her father had intended for her female heirs. "I have no intention of obliging the gentlemen who make their profits on gaming at Tattersall's. Or elsewhere. It would be a shameful trick against Mr. Kyle."

Kinsham said, "Oh? Then your concern is for the noble Stephen. Not the morality of the wager itself."

She shrugged. "I have won and lost wagers before. Two years ago I wagered against you and half the court on Lady

95

Bessborough's influence with Prinny. You were all so sure he would break with her. And of course, you won.''

"If you want to win back your losses, I suggest you watch the demon duchess and try to outface her. She intends to purchase a property of some sort in Sussex. Darking Hill, it seems to me. As near your Stephen Kyle as makes no matter. She intends to win your wager."

The knowledge shook her far more than she believed possible, but she had no intention of letting Vincent Kinsham guess the truth.

Martin Dalreagh had insisted upon a splendid wedding dinner, which involved two main courses with enough dishes to feed an entire country, as the new Countess Elfreda pointed out a trifle tartly, but she had been outvoted by her husband and her father who both enjoyed their food. Each elaborately prepared dish was succeeded by one even richer and more splendidly served. Always impressed by such expenditures, the "Dowager" Countess heartily concurred, though the dishes themselves, needing a light French touch, were not always as successful as one might have hoped.

The Dowager Countess said, "Such a dinner should be elaborate. It will, perhaps, make one forget that paltry wedding."

"I thought it was a very—efficient wedding," Favia remarked, choosing the only suitable adjective she could think of at the moment.

Her defense of the wedding had not prevented her from asking Beckett to bring out a new silk evening gown of the modern short length that revealed her instep. The gown, with its fashionably short puffed sleeves, was banded over and under the bosom and around the hem with deep rose satin. She did not go to the formal extreme of wearing the white feathers in her hair that a dinner with His Highness would have required, but Vincent Kinsham seemed to exaggerate his flattery, and she wished she had taken less care with her toilette.

She need not have concerned herself with what the bride might think. The new Countess Elfreda, still wearing her high-necked, unpretentious bridal gown, casually agreed with the viscount. "Cousin Favia always looks lovely. Have you tried the mutton cutlets? I note you avoid the turtle soup. It's a great favorite with Papa, and you may discern just a hint of—I rather fancy it's Madeira."

"Sherry," her father put in. He had served the Dowager with great care and remarked with more romance than originality that she ate like a bird. Now he settled down to enjoy his beloved turtle soup before he plunged into his plate of tongue, fricassee of chicken, creamed onions, and boiled potatoes. He washed everything down with hock while admirably managing to give the Dowager Countess all the attention she expected.

If Favia had followed her real inclinations, she would have left Dalreagh an hour after the wedding ceremony. She told herself that she could move as rapidly as Stephen Kyle. But Kyle was rushing to join a loved one who needed him. Favia felt that she would be deserting her own nearest relation, her mother, just when the countess faced her first shattering days as "the Dowager" of Dalreagh.

During these hours, however, it began to be clear that Sir Julius Worthingham would console the Dowager Countess for her loss of prestige. He proved to be surprisingly adept at this art and his attentions were welcomed by the flattered lady. Whenever the titles of the new earl and his countess were accentuated by the wedding guests, the neighbors from Bath, Wells, and the countryside, Sir Julius used his cherubic charm to address the Dowager very audibly as "Her Ladyship, the countess."

On the second night Favia mentioned a possible return to Brighton with the perfectly true excuse that His Highness, the Regent, had asked the two Dalreagh ladies to act as his hostesses at a Pavilion Ball for the young Princess of Wales. Since the Prince seldom put himself to the trouble of entertaining his daughter and heir, it was an impressive excuse. Favia had been less than candid about the date, however, which was actually more than a fortnight hence.

Only Vincent Kinsham knew the truth about the date, and the viscount was far too interested in the outcome of the supposed wager between Favia and Beatrix Hungerford to interfere with whatever stratagems she employed.

Her stratagem was simple. She dressed with Lady Favia Dalreagh's own usual care, striving for elegance without the bizarre look of Beatrix Hungerford. She had determined to find Stephen Kyle, pursue him to his home, if necessary. She would then show him herself as she really was and remind him that it was he who first assumed she was a serving woman.

He was notoriously anxious to be fair to the poor, the wretched, and the victims of injustice. Couldn't he expend some of that charity on a young woman whose only real crime was he membership in a class he professed to despise? She would not plead for his understanding or forgiveness. She was determined to meet him on his own level, but perhaps with a quiet, gentle pride that would move him to regard her fairly. Being an opinionated and lively young woman, she was not usually noted for her "quiet gentleness" but doubtless those qualities would appear when she needed them.

The next morning Lady Favia Dalreagh left the wedding party in the older Dalreagh coach with Hibbings, the under-coachman on the box, and an armed footman as outrider. She had no other abigail properly trained, so Libbie Beckett was pressed into service. She had decided to introduce the real Beckett to Kyle as well as herself. That would certainly demonstrate her wish to rectify any suggestion of deceit. Now that the Duchess of Hungerford had made it so easy to provide a plausible excuse for her visit to Sussex, Favia would simply say that she was on her way to stay a few days with "her friend, the duchess." That would be turning the tables on Beatrix with a vengeance!

On her way to Sussex she planned on spending only one night in Brighton. There she would ask for an audience with His Highness, the Prince Regent, and explain that the entire wager was a jest created by the Duchess of Hungerford and Viscount Kinsham.

His Highness might be cross with the real perpetrators of a distasteful wager, but it was also possible that he would resent her own role in destroying a wager he enjoyed. She was willing to chance it. Indeed, she must, if she was to face Stephen Kyle with what might be called "clean hands."

But unfortunately her plans concerning the Regent could not be carried out in her own person, as she had hoped. She learned from Miss Durrance, her mother's companion, that Prinny was no longer in Brighton.

"Oh, Your Ladyship," exclaimed Miss Durrance, "I vow, I was that surprised when I heard the gossip. His Highness hurried—actually hurried off to London to avoid his wife's visit to Brighton. It is the merest hint. We've no definite word. But there it is. His Highness is no longer in Brighton."

It was maddening. Favia knew she must rely upon her own messenger to reach His Highness at Carlton House, if, indeed, he had gone to earth at his London address. She was not at all certain she could persuade him to abandon the affair of the wager, by the act of pen and paper.

Still, it must be done.

She knew he was too impatient to read a long and involved plea. She thought about the wording of the letter, the fewest possible phrases, and finally resorted to the obvious winning argument: Her Highness, the Princess Caroline (his hated wife), was enthusiastic over the supposed wager, and though Favia had pleaded that the idea was absurd, Her Highness insisted that the wager be officially recorded.

To give her argument added force, Favia wrote that when she had pleaded to cancel the wager Her Highness had announced, "With her expressed interest no one would dare to cancel it."

"If that doesn't rouse him, nothing will," Favia told herself and impressed the Dalreagh seal upon the folded sheet.

There was only one servant she trusted to carry the message up to London. Young Biddlecomb, the footman who had served as an outrider on the journey to Brighton, was known to His Highness and even to some of the Carlton House servants. He wouldn't have as much difficulty getting her message to one of His Highness's secretaries.

This meant that only Hibbings and Libbie Beckett would accompany her to Sussex, but the journey was not a long one. Surely not too many disasters could befall a resourceful woman of initiative and confidence. It might even impress Stephen Kyle with her democratic habits.

Libbie Beckett objected in her plaintive, vaguely whining voice when Favia decided not to take several of her jewel sets.

"But, ma'am, they'll be thinking you're such a dowd,"

she insisted. "You ought to be taking the rubies and that great parure set of diamonds. They do sparkle so."

"Now, where would I wear such a set in a rural Sussex town."

Beckett persisted. "But the rubies! Do say you'll take them."

"They do not suit the small wardrobe I am taking. Besides, I am not in my best looks with rubies."

"Oh, but, ma'am, everyone looks good in—"

"That will do, Beckett."

She subsided. "Well, then, if you say, ma'am, I'll just tuck the packet away in your big case for safekeeping."

In the maple-framed mirror set on top of the highboy Favia caught the acquisitive gleam in Beckett's eyes and said casually, "No. I will attend to it. Run along and see if Hibbings understands we are to make an early start."

Beckett, who seemed to have enchanted the dour Hibbings in their brief journey from home to Brighton, ran to obey, but not without several backward glances at the rejected rubies. As usual, she must have spent considerable time charming the coachman. She did not return for nearly an hour.

The following day, after Miss Durrance's promise to "deny with amused contempt" any talk of the dishonorable wager, Favia and Beckett left Brighton in the old, unfashionable coach with its worn velvet fittings and sturdy team. Beckett's expression clearly revealed her disgust for such conditions, but the little coachman was surprisingly amenable when he discovered he would have no postboys or an outrider of any sort. He must mange turnpikes, tollgates, and accidents of the road with whatever authority Favia delegated to him.

This served surprisingly well the few posting houses properly daunted by Lady Favia Dalreagh's cool, pleasant manner in issuing orders, or possibly impressed by her overpayments. She might be "sporting the blunt" a bit too freely, as Vincent Kinsham often proclaimed, but she had learned long ago the value of a few shillings properly distributed.

Conversation with Beckett eventually became a monologue. The girl was uncharacteristically silent. When Favia asked if the swaying of the coach made her ill, she denied this. All the same, she could not seem to sit still. She kept leaning forward to peer out the window as the day wore on, and to inquire anxiously if Her Ladyship often traveled by night.

Favia was just congratulating herself that their journey had gone remarkably well with none of the usual highroad mishaps when their luck turned. Having traveled some distance along the busy London Post Road by accident, Hibbings was forced to turn off in the afternoon and rattle across the Sussex marshes past the distant Cinque Port of Royal Rye toward the village that crowned the sharp rise of Darking Hill.

Favia had never been more tired of the coach's dusty, airless interior. She let down the window and gazed eastward toward the marshes with their curious look of a landscape on the moon, lacking humanity or anything else that moved. She knew this was a false impression. The marshes were very much alive with sheep whose wool had furnished the chief object of trade for French brandy during the past six hundred and more years.

By this hour the sky over the distant waters of the English Channel had turned a foggy pink. Against this background the small eminence of Darking Hill looked strangely unreal. The hill itself was nearly surrounded by marshy inlets from the Channel, which might explain why the village began to creep over the top of the hill from halfway up the steep slopes.

Libbie Beckett peered out from her side of the racketing coach and murmured thoughtfully, "we're that near on the coast; I wouldn't have believed it." She drew her head in abruptly. "Ma'am, Hibbings is signing to me about some'ut . . . something." At the same time the carriage jolted back and forth, then halted. Beckett added as Favia looked out again, "What luck, ma'am! There's a coteen yonder. And there's a lantern swinging from a hook. It's a posting house, most like."

"Let us be grateful for small favors." If, indeed, the aging, squat stone house could be said to resemble even a very obscure posting house! There seemed to be a half story set above the ground floor and punctured by three crooked dormer windows uneasily set in the low roof. The only light, as Beckett noted, glimmered smokily in a lantern beside the door.

Meanwhile, Hibbings had climbed down from the box somewhat laboriously and gone to settle the fractious team before returning to call out as he reached the door on Favia's side of the coach: "We've a bit of a problem, ma'am. There's that near wheel right there." He kicked at the forward wheel nearest Favia. It shivered under the blow. Favia knew very little about the mechanics of carriage wheels, but this unquestionably looked unsafe. It might even fall off the next time they rode over a hole in this badly rutted lane.

She took a deep, impatient breath. "Well, what are we to do? It can't be more than an hour to Darking Hill."

"True, but the sun being gone and all, Your La'ship must be needing a bit of supper. Maybe a sip of that good brandy they sneaks past the excisemen in these parts."

103

"And there's an inn, ma'am," Beckett reminded her eagerly. "It's like it was providential.

Favia looked around at the easterly horizon so quickly dissolving into the foggy mist that rose from the marshes. Toward the west the sun had already dipped behind rugged outcroppings, hillocks, and hills with an occasional farm or manor house silhouetted against the still-yellow sky. Nothing nearby except this wretched inn, if indeed, it was a public house. She nodded.

"See to the horses. Perhaps you can get the carriage as far as the house. Come along, Beckett."

Beckett was clearly happy for any change from the rocking coach. She started out enthusiastically, marching over the ground toward the weed-grown patch that had once been a kitchen garden. Every step or two she looked over he shoulder to see if Favia was following. After taking up her small jewel case and stuffing it into a larger velvet and tapestry case, Favia came along, relieved that she had chosen her traveling gown, her green pelisse, and bonnet, so carefully. They were reasonably modest in style, so that the casual habitué of a wayside tavern would not guess at their great cost.

"Wait," she ordered Beckett, who reached for the weathered and heavily reinforced door of the old house. "Hibbings had best come in with us. Two women alone may give them a few nasty notions."

"Oh, ma'am, what an idea!"

Something—some curious thrill of excitement running through Beckett's voice—gave Favia her first genuine alarm. Her eyes narrowed, and she glanced around. Hibbings was unexpectedly close. He must have left the team standing and hurried after the two women. With a little added height he might be breathing upon her bonnet rather than the nape of her neck.

Ignoring her, Beckett was already pushing the door open. Favia repeated "I said—!" when the door opened from within. She glimpsed the ill-lighted taproom of what appeared to be a genuine tavern. The individual in the doorway was bulky, coarse-featured, perhaps a prize-fighter, judging by the peculiar break across the bridge of his broad, deeply colored nose. He was belted somewhat tightly into a shiny tan jerkin that might have graced a frontiersman in the New World. Homespun sleeves did not conceal his scarred fists.

He seemed all too pleased to see Libbie Beckett. "So, ye're here at last, my pretty doxy," he greeted the nervous abigail.

Favia found herself so angry at being led into this trap that she nearly lost all fear. "A friend of yours, Beckett? Pray introduce him. A smuggler, I make no doubt."

The hulking fellow presented himself, complete with a deep bow. His movements helped to spread the stench of spirits through the air. "Not a smuggler, lass. Not Lemuel Peeber. The highroad's my lay. And this here little doxy, she run away, all account of a wee tap on the jaw, friendly-like. But all's well now. She's come home to old Lemuel. And with as pretty a bit of profit as those old eyes ever seen. Ay, ma'am, you'll be worth the effort and no mistake."

CHAPTER NINE

With every sinew aware, Favia managed a reasonably pleasant smile. She hoped to keep the fellow from violence by conversation while she gave half her brain the task of finding a way out. Two roughly clad men had been lounging on the stiff, unpadded settles at right angles to the peat fire in the fireplace. One of these men looked scarcely old enough to shave. His moon face glistened in the firelight when he turned to watch her. He was big-eyed with curiosity, and his mouth hung open loosely.

The other man, well on in years, perhaps fifty, appeared to be an outdoor man, his face burned a rough red by the sun and wind. In these marshes so near the Channel he was very likely an ex-seaman of some kind. He wore an old-fashioned black tricorne hat pushed far back on his thick, grizzled head of hair, and he did not look like a murderer, which was one point of relief. Still, only time and luck would tell. Both men obviously belonged to Lemuel Peeber's band of highwaymen.

Favia forced herself not to appear as apprehensive as she felt. "So, you are Beckett's friend, Captain Peeber," she began, giving him the usual title sported by highwaymen. "You must be responsible for her rare skill. I assure you I have noted it. Such light fingers! Are you also acquainted with the Kyle family? I believe Miss Selina has often befriended your—'' She was about to say ''kind'' but amended it. ''—your comrades.''

Only Hibbings was undisturbed. He had placed himself in front of the door and leaned back against it as though he were a mere spectator.

On the others the name made the disturbance she hoped for. The two men on the settles straightened up, set there booted feet on the floor. Without looking around at them, Lemuel Peeber waved them and Libbie Beckett to silence. ''So, you're a friend to Master Steve! A likely lad. He'd strip to advantage in the ring. . . .'' He hesitated, glanced at Beckett, who shrugged. Then he asked with interest, ''This Master Kyle, he's hereabouts, maybe in hopes of meeting Your Ladyship?''

Hibbings put in, ''That's in the right of it, Cap'n. Her La'ship come to visit Master Kyle. They're friends-like.''

Secretly thanking the coachman for his gratuitous information, Favia smiled warmly in Peeber's toothy face. ''Just so. Master Kyle's sister, Miss Selina, has invited me for a visit in the name of our old friendship, and Stephen—I mean to say, Mr. Kyle—will meet my coach at any minute. The team is well-known to him. The right wheeler was a gift to my mother from the dear fellow.''

The older man by the fire cleared his throat and reached for a spill to light his pipe. Lemuel Peeber scowled at him. ''Quiet, Bucko! Our Parliamentary friend, he's been off to Rye. He's not due to pass for hours. We'll be long on our way before midnight. Libbie, take Her Ladyship's valise.''

''There's a bigger one in the coach,'' Hibbings said.

Beckett scrambled for Favia's valise, confused when Favia offered it with a smile whose edges were sardonic. ''Are you happy now, Beckett? You always wanted it.''

Lemuel Peeber snatched the valise from Beckett, who complained with a voice close to tears, "She wouldn't bring the rubies. Not even one earbob. No rubies. Or the big diamond set. Or—or—"

She was silenced by Lemuel Peeber. "You're a greedy little doxy, m'dear. You—Hibbert? Hibbings? Fetch in the lady's other luggage."

Hibbings gave them all one of his narrowed, lizard looks, then scuttled out, closing the door gently. The man by the fire said, "Do we have to deal with dogs like that? You blind and deaf, Peeber? You know how she got that creetur to betray the lady."

Hoping to win an unexpected friend, Favia tried to express her gratitude in a look. Meanwhile Libbie Beckett rudely fingered Favia's bonnet and then, as Favia tossed her head, shaking off her touch, the girl's hand dropped to the sleeve of the green shot-silk pelisse.

"I'll have this. And this," the girl insisted, running her tongue over her teeth in anticipation.

Favia let her fingers prowl greedily along the rich material, while she herself edged back against the door. Part of her attention was distracted by hopeful signs of dispute between Captain Peeber and the man by the fire, the seaman called "Bucko," who moved toward him until they were arguing in what was little above a whisper. Favia had no doubt that she was its subject.

It occurred to her that this might be her only chance of escape. She fumbled behind her for the edge of the door, which was still ajar, and had pulled it open an inch of two when it was suddenly pushed hard against her body, and she stumbled forward into Libbie Beckett. Beckett screamed out a few phrases astonishing from so demure a mouth, but Hibbings had come back from the coach with Favia's band-box, her portmanteaus, and even a narrow box in which two gowns for festive rural evenings had been stored.

This effectively silenced Beckett's cursing complaints. She snatched at two portmanteaus and dragged them across the floor. While she was prying them open, the boy left the settle and fumbled at Peeber's arm. "Best begone, Cap'n. There's no time. No time a'tall."

"We're got what we're here for," Bucko insisted. "Let your doxy take the fal-lals, and we'll be off with Her Ladyship's jewels."

Peeber grinned at Favia. She guessed that he was aware of her furtive attempts to slip out the door, now that Hibbings had joined Libbie Beckett in examining her property. She remained absolutely still under his curious stare, but within she seethed with anger and indignation.

Peeber kicked over the small jewel box Libbie Beckett had discarded. Amid the silver paper and soft satin cushions many of her jewels glittered in the light from the rich, heavy branch of tallow candles at one end of the taproom bar. Peeber nodded, rubbing the stubble on his chin.

"You've done well, Libbie. Like you promised when you sent your friend Hibbings to us. Hibbings, my lad, you're cut in for shares."

"Share out, then, and let's be gone," Bucko insisted while Hibbings nodded hungrily. He had lifted several strands of pearls and was running them through his fingers, their pink opalescence reminding Favia of the day her grandmother had dropped them about her neck on her sixteenth birthday. How proud she had been, and how she loved them because of their beloved giver!

But she would not beg. That creature, Libbie Beckett, would never see her beg. Of them all it was the abigail she hated most profoundly and resolved not to show her any pity when the reckoning came. She never doubted there would be a reckoning. She moved stealthily backward. Peeber was not fooled.

"Hibbings, pile it all into the cases, and take them out. Alfie—" He turned to the nervous boy. "You lend him that spindly arm of yours. Libbie, you, too. Hibbings, you got the wheel on solid?"

"Solid, Captain. It's my business to keep tight rein on a coach wheel."

Libbie had been squatting ungracefully among the jewels and the other contents of Favia's luggage. She jumped to her feet now, her hands filled with Favia's property.

"I want what she's wearing, Lemuel. I come back to you for all the pretty fal-lals, and you vowed—"

The amiable Peeber agreed. "Ay, lass. You shall have them. Here. Bucko, give aid to Hibbings. I'll see to the lady."

"That you will not," Beckett insisted, but Peeber scarcely heard her. His long, apelike arms caught Favia as she was about to slip out the open door. He dragged her to him, pulling off her bonnet while she struggled, kicked with all her considerable strength, catching him on the kneecap so that he yelled, called her a "hell-kite!" and commanded someone over her head, "Fetch me ropes. Tackle. Anything. Damn the creature!"

With her head smotheringly pressed against the deerskin jerkin, which stank of gin and the captain's unwashed body, Favia continued her wild, unthinking struggle. It was motivated as much against the indignity of this ridiculous business as against the more obvious dangers.

She was the center of a furore. That creature, Libbie Beckett, continued to pull at her. The pelisse was already off one shoulder and arm. The highwayman lifted her off her feet. She continued to make herself prickly and painful to Peebers as to anyone who touched her.

110

Nevertheless, she recognized the voice of the seaman called Bucko. "Set the lady down, Peeber. Jesu! We ain't damned pirates. Nor cutthroats, come to that. Your doxy's got enough loot."

Hibbings, too, had returned, calling from the door, "Cap'n, we're ready. No time to lose. There's the Rye and Hastings stage coming. She's hours late."

"See her?"

"I saw the coach lights off the foot of Rye Hill. I know the look of 'em."

Slipping from Peeber's hands, Favia tumbled to the floor, where she lay a minute of two, breathless with shock. All about her there was a great scurrying. Someone, undoubtedly Libbie Beckett, began to tug at the right sleeve of her pelisse. Favia kicked out, felt the ghastly softness of flesh, and was almost pleased by Libbie Beckett's shriek of pain and rage. The girl struck at Favia, hitting her above the ribs and tentatively knocking the breath from her. Doubtless she would have done more, but someone lifted the girl away, and after an interminable minute or so Favia's wrists were drawn together and bound with something rough, probably hemp.

"Tighter," Peeber ordered. "You're too easy." She supposed either Bucko or the boy was tying her hands, and more gently than Peeber would have treated her.

She protested at the cloth Peeber stuffed into her mouth, but this was not the end of her indignities. Someone dropped a loose-woven sack over her head, and she was thrown hard against the wall behind the tapster's bar.

Confused and half-stifled, with her head ringing painfully, she still retained enough common sense to understand that the gang was leaving without having murdered her. She supposed that she might call herself lucky.

Someone snuffed the candles, the door slammed, and she

111

heard a brief argument because the hasp was broken and the door would not lock. The room was left in a lurid dark-and-brightness from the intermittent sparks in the fireplace.

The night was still. Despite the stifling warm air inside the sack, Favia's hands, which were outside the sack, began to grow cold, then prickling, and finally numb. She shook her fingers vigorously, while her tongue and teeth attempted to work the cloth out of her mouth. She suspected the cloth, with its rank and dusty taste, had been used by the tapster to wipe off the bar. Its probable filth seemed more horrible than the knock on her head.

The tapster. Where was he?

She wriggled toward the hearth, feeling along the warm floor to give her some kind of direction. The rope that bound her wrists was somewhat eased. She wondered if Bucko had deliberately made it easier for her. Meanwhile the cloth caused her to cough and choke. She managed to get about half of it out, which relieved her slightly, but the exertion made her head feel as if it would burst. Instinctively she felt that she must not go to sleep, but her eyes closed in spite of herself, and she sensed that time was slipping by.

Once, hoofbeats and the rattle of harness told her that very likely the Rye to Hastings stage was approaching. She tried to scream but heard only the rasp and gurgle of noise that would hardly attract the wildly racketing stage. In any case, this wretched inn was not one of the stops. The stage rolled by, undoubtedly attempting to make up time after the mishap that had delayed its regular run.

Having listened with enormous tension until the last echoes had died away along the road, she found her head bursting. The only relief came when she closed her eyes. She might thank Libbie Beckett for the blow that seemed to be tearing her head apart at this minute. But there were

112

many things for which she might thank the little abigail—her predicament in this hellish place, for example.

With her eyes closed to relieve the pressure of her aching head, she tried to concentrate on releasing her hands at the same time that she spat and coughed over the choking cloth.

She could not imagine how she slept in such circumstances, but when she regained consciousness sometime later, the fire had died down to ashes. She seemed to be stifling and realized she must have awakened herself by her choking.

Or were there other sounds? She listened, hearing the thump of her own heartbeat and her heavy, gasping breaths. More than that. Sounds farther away. Hoofbeats, and this time made by a single horse. In spite of Hibbings's warning, it was too much to hope that this might be Stephen Kyle returning from Rye. But almost anyone would be welcome. Ignoring a persistently aching head, she began to move again, hoping she could escape from behind the tapster's bar and be seen in spite of the semidarkness.

She stopped a minute or two later and listened again. The horseman was much nearer. Let him stop. . . . Let him—

The pelt of horse's hooves went on, passing the inn. There were no lights about the place. Small wonder. Her muscles relaxed with the hopelessness of her position. *I must free myself. There is no other way.*

She wrestled again with the ropes around her wrists. The flesh felt badly bruised, but this was a small matter if she could free herself. Another sound made her stiffen with both hope and fear. What if this might be another criminal, a highwayman or a smuggler? The rider had dismounted. She heard the squeal of the front door as it was pushed open.

Stephen Kyle's voice. She could not mistake that light,

113

half-joking tone that overlay the unmistakable level of authority. "Jude! Your storm light is out. As a matter of fact, this taproom— Is anyone here?"

She made every sound she could think of, coughing, clearing her throat, thumping the floor with her heels and her still-bound hands.

She heard him striding across the room. A minute later, through the rough sacking over her head, she guessed that he had lighted the candle branch from a spill on the hearth. He must have been looking around, perhaps up the rickety stairs at the far end of the room, before he came back toward the tapster's bar and saw her.

"Good God!" She felt herself lifted up to the settle and the sack removed from her head. If her head hadn't ached so much, she might have laughed at his expression as he recognized her. "Libbie Beckett!"

She winced and grunted. He began to pull the cloth out of her mouth. "My dear girl—how the devil—? What happened here?" She tried to speak, but nothing came out of her dry, sore mouth except grunts from her throat.

He put his arms around her body, reaching behind her to free her wrists. "What were you doing here? Do you know Jude? Why aren't you at Dalreagh?"

With her hands free she flexed her fingers painfully. He took her hands in his and began to rub them between his fingers while he looked around her head, obviously expecting to see his friend Jude appear at any second, perhaps in her condition.

She tried again to speak, but the croaking sounds that came forth embarrassed her, and she was still unsure of how she would explain her true identity to him.

He asked her if she felt "easier." When she nodded, she saw that half his thoughts were occupied with the mystery of his friend Jude. "He is a good fellow, you know.

Has a rough custom here, with what we call 'the gentlemen' coming through this road often enough. Smugglers, you understand. Were they responsible for your mistreatment? If they were, you may believe they will be punished. Was it smuggler? I believe I know all of them."

She shook her head.

He frowned. "Just ruffians of the road, I take it."

She shrugged.

She had hoped for his sympathy, but she was a little afraid and even disappointed at the way he looked at her now. In her confused state she could not understand why he seemed suspicious. She tried to get an explanation out but heard once more the embarrassing, dry-mouthed sounds. He ran one finger over her lips in a tantalizing, tempting gesture and said, "Never mind. Jude knows every smuggler along the coast. I daresay, he has allowed himself to be bound like you. He would have a difficult time explaining his condition otherwise. Our local excisemen are persistent."

She did not know what else to do and could say nothing intelligible, so she merely nodded. Stephen Kyle looked at her for a long moment. "Are you feeling better now?"

It was a teasing, whimsical question, and she managed to croak, "Yes."

"The fellows who did this. Are you certain they are gone?"

She nodded, adding "coach." It was the only word she could get out. Her tongue felt dry and yet so swelled she was sure she would never be able to use it again.

He removed his hands from her shoulders, told her, "Rest. Breathe deeply. You will soon by yourself again. I am going to find Jude Maskel. He may have been knocked unconscious. If you hear anything outside, any sound at all, call me. Can you do that?"

She nodded, but her head was thumping with pain, and she did not feel as concerned over the unseen, unknown Jude Maskel as she might have done in ordinary circumstances. She watched Kyle cross the room toward the old staircase, admiring as always the easy grace with which he moved. She knew her own reactions were absurd. He had very little interest in her and still seemed obsessed with the idea that she was an abigail named "Libbie Beckett."

Holding her head between her bruised hands, she got up and followed him to the foot of the stairs beyond the wall of the taproom. He disappeared upstairs into one of the rooms under the steep, slanting roof. She heard him call out Jude's name in a questioning tone that made her more uneasy, for no one answered, nor were there any sounds.

Several minutes went by. When she heard his footsteps again on the creaking floor overhead, she realized his friend, the innkeeper, must have left the inn untended. For the first time she wondered seriously where Jude Maskel had gone.

Stephen Kyle reappeared at the top of the stairs, looking down at her. Even in the dusky shadows she could see his face, the features strong and firm, yet she sensed the tension about him. She started up anxiously.

"No! Stay there." He snapped it out like a military order, but she was not offended. She knew at once that he must have found his friend. The cold of the night and the foggy marshlands crept over her body.

She managed to whisper, "You found him? Dead?"

"Choked to death on the rag they stuffed into his mouth, if I'm any judge. He was bound hand and foot."

She cried out, but he had reached her by now and pulled her to him with her cheek against his throat, his arms holding her securely against his body. "Here, my lass. You've been a brave girl. Don't give up."

116

"Not that," she complained hoarsely. "Just my head."

Holding her upright with one arm, he ran the fingers of his other hand through her tousled hair. She winced. He found the source of her trouble in a rapidly rising lump above her left temple. At least, he did not ask the non-sensical question: "Does that hurt?" Frowning, he raised her chin and studied her eyes. Her eyelids felt heavy, and she blinked. Suddenly, adding further to her confusion, he lifted her off her feet and into his arms.

Afterward she remembered an instant of regret that she couldn't enjoy this attention; then her eyes closed, and she lost consciousness.

CHAPTER TEN

Freshly laundered curtains enclosed the heavy four-poster bed. Thin curtains filtered the sun through. Staring at that light, Favia realized that she was definitely not lying in one of the attic rooms of Jude Maskel's inn.

She roused herself, leaning back on her elbows to get a better look out the two casement windows across the room. In some respects it reminded her of the Brighton house rather than Dalreagh, where every window opened upon trees, greenery, or the meandering brook. Here there appeared to be nothing but a bright sky flecked with clouds beyond the window, from which she gathered that the low-growing marshes lay below and beyond the window. This did not appear to be the ground floor. Could this be Stephen Kyle's house on Darking Hill?

She cleared her throat and tried to speak. Her voice seemed to have recovered its normal, pleasant timbre. "Is anyone here?"

Her movements had uncovered her body, she discovered that she was wearing a night rail much too big for her, a gown with long, full sleeves and a high neckline whose lace frill scratched her throat. Remarkable unbecoming, of a rough material more suited to the lining of a cloak than a bedgown. And the color was worse. She could think of it only as "puce," a shade she detested. But uninvited guests must not complain. Perhaps she had been brought to another inn, and this gown belonged to one of the servants.

Her head gave a nasty twinge as she exerted herself, and she felt for the injury over her temple. It was covered by a bandage, and the bandage by a night-bonnet that concealed almost all of her hair. She must look ghastly in it, but this was no time for considerations of vanity. She was grateful to Stephen Kyle and whoever had kindly given her shelter.

All of her means of identification had gone with her coach, horses, and stolen property, so her rescuers were clearly providing this comfortable room for "Libbie Beckett," the lady's maid. This argued a very generous and democratic rescuer. Stephen Kyle, of course. But she thought a woman must have a part in it. The bright and cheerful room was clearly feminine.

She groaned as further exertions produced pinpricking reminders of her headache last night. Or had it been only last night? Each of her wrists seemed to be confined. She turned back the long cuffs of the bedgown that covered her to the knuckles and saw that some Good Samaritan had bound each of her chafed and bruised wrists.

Studying the frill of the gown and the clean linen around her wrists, she decided that Stephen Kyle had turned her over to the most logical female, his sister. She was relieved that he had considered the proprieties enough to do so. Some gentlemen, believing her to be an unprotected and defenseless servant, would have behaved in a very different manner.

She tried to speak again, actually expecting no answer but anxious to test her voice. "Where the deuce am I?"

119

It was not the highly proper language she might have used had she expected to be overheard, and she was startled with a gruff, far from conciliatory voice snapped, "Darking Hill, my girl. What were you expecting, indeed?"

"Good heavens!" She sat up and pushed aside the curtains. "Where are you?"

"Under your nose, girl. Under your nose." The scrape of a straight-backed armchair behind the bed, near the hall door, gave Favia the proper direction, and she pushed the bed curtains further aside.

A tall, vigorous female of an advanced age, certainly over Stephen Kyle's midthirties, rose from the armchair and limped toward the bed. She bore a distinct resemblance to Stephen, but the aquiline nose, the gray eyes, and firm mouth with its small quirk of humor that made the male so attractive gave Miss Selina a forbidding aspect.

She looked down at her guest and sniffed. "Looking more the thing, I see. Nasty blow you had there. I daresay, it was a gift from those friends of yours."

"I am not likely to befriend murderous highwaymen, Miss Selina."

The lady's tawny eyebrows went up. "You know me, then." She laughed shortly. It was more of a snort and made Favia smile, though she covered her mouth quickly.

"I could not mistake the resemblance to your brother."

"Quite so." Miss Selina gave her reflection a brief survey in the gilt-framed mirror on the right-hand wall. "But you would do better to say he resembles me, since I was very much alive when Stephen came into the world. But that is neither here nor there." She looked Favia over critically. "my night rail does not flatter you. No matter. We have one thing in common, young Libbie."

"Miss Kyle, I must correct you. I am not—" But The lady's voice overrode the attempt to identify herself.

120

"Consider. We have both been wronged by the family of Dalreagh."

Favia was so startled she scarcely understood this flat statement. "Your pardon, ma'am. You—you are acquainted with the Dalreaghs?"

"Acquainted?" she snapped. "You may call it so. Aye. And lucky for you, Libbie Beckett, else I'd have turned you out on the marshes, injuries or not. I don't hold with females waylaying poor travelers, helping to slit their throats, and strangling innkeepers, like as not."

"But I wasn't helping anyone slit—"

Miss Selina held up one large, well-shaped hand. "My brother tells me you have been mistreated in the service of the Dalreaghs. I am given to understand that you were accused of theft and other crimes for which you might be hanged."

"No!"

"Or, at the very least, deported to the antipodes. And all through the caprice of that monstrous daughter of a monstrous family. In truth, it is they who should be hanged," she amended in a way that did not reassure Favia, "or at all events, transported."

Stunned, Favia sank back among the pillows. Her head began to ache again, and she raised her hand, feeling the bandage beneath the absurd nightcap. What would this woman do to her if she discovered Favia's true identity? She managed a totally inadequate reply, "I am persuaded Her Ladyship meant no harm."

"Your charity does you credit, girl. But it will not eradicate memories of unspeakable cruelty."

What can the Dalreaghs have done to provoke such bitterness? Favia wondered. She was wildly curious to know, and yet she sensed that too many questions might draw the wrong attention to her. She could only pray that no one of her acquaintance at court would wander into the village of Darking Hill until she was gone.

"But, miss—that is—ma'am, I assure you, I parted from the Dalreagh service only because Lady Favia's abigail returned to her post. They could scarcely afford the expense of two abigails for Her Ladyship."

"Penny-pinching, besides all else."

Favia gave up the subject. She began to revise her plans. It seemed now that she must continue to play "Libbie Beckett," at least until she was feeling more the thing. If she could discover what great crimes had been committed against the Kyle family by the Dalreaghs, she would better respond to the accusations.

Meanwhile she might find it a trifle difficult to continue her subservient role. This expedition, which had started so easily, almost as a game, was beginning to tax her acting ability. She was much too assertive and would have to watch such small matters as addressing Selina Kyle by the respectful title of "ma'am" rather than in the manner of an equal.

She wondered how her position as an unemployed abigail could be woven into the story of her presence at the inn. What was she, in the role of "Libbie Beckett," doing in the company of scoundrels like Captain Lemuel Peeber and his associates?

"Now, then," Miss Selina went on brusquely, "your hands, do they pain you?"

Favia examined the bandages on her wrists. "No, ma'am," she added as a sop to sweeten the woman's abrasive disposition, "it was splendid of you. I mean to say, so very kind."

Miss Selina towered over the bed in a most intimidating fashion. She plumped up one of the pillows behind Favia's head and then, with an excess of energy, shook the bed-curtains, which made Favia sneeze.

"Kind it was, but no work of mine. My talents run in other directions. Isaiah Micklehouse played the surgeon, and made good work of it. Excellent fellow, Isaiah. Was used to be a smuggler. What we hereabouts call 'one of the gentlemen.' "

Favia rolled her eyes toward the crossbeam in the ceiling. It was all that had been needed, that smugglers should be attending her while she was unconscious! She stirred and tried to sit up again, groaning at the effort it cost her. She ached in every bone and sinew.

Seeing her discomfort, Miss Selina went to the door and called, "Isaiah! Where are you? Lying about, I make no doubt. Drat the man!"

To protest seemed futile. The lady looked as though she were quite capable of commanding a smuggler. She and her brother would probably have been more than a match for Lemuel Peeber and his cutthroats. Favia turned and watched for Isaiah Micklehouse, expecting the worst, a ruffian like Peeber.

Voices in the hall told her that Stephen Kyle accompanied Isaiah, that smuggler with the surgical touch. Favia tried to pull herself into some kind of order in the few seconds left to her before they came in. Stephen asked his sister, "How is she? Is she herself now? That must have been a rough blow on the head. I suppose they all fell out over the jewels the girl had taken from the Dalreagh women. Still, she hardly deserved to be voted out of the gang with such enthusiasm."

How did he know about the jewels? Favia wondered. He seemed omniscient in many ways, though he still hadn't guessed her identity. At the same time the Kyles and their acquaintances had an extraordinary idea of criminality.

They consorted with smugglers and welcomed Favia into their house. They took excellent care of her injuries, and permitted her to lie in one of their loveliest bedchambers, although they suspected her of being a thief, consort of a band of cutthroats. Their moral notions were peculiar, to say the least.

Still, Stephen Kyle had saved her. Judging by the fate of the unfortunate Jude Maskel, he might be said to have saved her life. That is to say, "Libbie Beckett" 's life. What on earth would he do to her when he discovered she was that hated creature, Lady Favia Dalreagh? She was still racking her brain to discover what awful crime had been committed by her family against his.

Miss Selina had waved the men into the room, and showing no sense of proper behavior, stalked out, leaving Favia unchaperoned in bed, surrounded by two males, one a rough smuggler. Stephen Kyle had never looked more attractive, in a homespun shirt, buckskin breeches, and boots that were well-fitted but much worn. They had probably not seen the fashionable champagne gloss in months, in ever. The shirt, open at the neck and revealing the tanned column of his throat, made him look especially exciting to her.

She became conscious of her own absurd looks and slipped down beneath the sheets, trying to cover herself. But there was no way of covering that ridiculous cap. She was hardly relieved by the amusement in Stephen's face as he studied her in her nest of pillows and bedclothing.

"Good day, Libbie. Feeling better in the sunlight? That was a long sleep. You had us worried. Kept us up most of the night, too. What do you think, Isaiah?"

While he was looking down at her, the smuggler, a stocky, white-haired man with an ingratiating grin, took up one of her wrists, poked at it with his thumb, and upon her indignant "Really!" he dropped that hand and picked up the other.

"Mighty pretty shape, sir. But I can see, ye've took note of that yourself."

"Don't embarrass the girl, Isaiah. Have you no manners? She will think she has merely exchanged her old friend, the cutthroat, for his mirror image."

All the same, Favia noted with mixed emotions that Stephen Kyle picked up her abandoned fingers and held them in his palm while he ran the forefinger of his other hand over them, as if to examine them in detail. It was, of course, an outrageous liberty, and Favia knew she must snatch her hand away at once or give him and his smuggler friend some very odd ideas of her character. She did so, but not before she acknowledged to herself that the sensation of his touch was highly enjoyable. She said caustically, "I daresay, there is little to choose between the two of you, if we come to that."

Stephen laughed. "Never mind. Isaiah will see to your injuries. I am here on a different matter." Despite that laugh, she thought his expression about the eyes had taken on a hardness that put her on her guard.

Remembering her supposed identity, she said meekly, "Yes, sir?" hoping to chase away what promised to be some awkward questions. She did not often play the meek, subservient little creature and was not entirely surprised when his voice roughened.

"Don't think to hoax me, you baggage! What are your relations with Lemuel Peeber? Were you his mistress?"

She rose up in bed, shocked at this preposterous suggestion. "Certainly not! How can you think I would consort with that filthy animal?"

"There'll be your answer, sir," Isaiah Micklehouse put in as he leaned over the bed to examine the bandage above

125

her left temple. With all his attention apparently devoted to her injury, he managed to add, "Don't look like any highwayman's doxy to me. But, howsoever, you might have closer dealings with such like, sir. You'd know better than me."

Trying to hide her anxiety, Favia looked from one to the other, waiting for Stephen Kyle's reaction. He frowned but ruined the effort at severity by the beginnings of a smile. "You may be right, Isaiah, your own life having been so sheltered. However, as you say, I am afraid this particular doxy must answer one or two questions or be turned over to the proper authorities."

"Shouldn't be too hard, sir, you being the justice of the peace, and that." Her eyes opened wide. Then she flinched as Isaiah pressed his thumb against the bump on her head. "I collect that as a justice of the peace you gather information by a little carelessly applied torture."

"Never carelessly applied," Stephen assured. "Everything, every stroke of the cat, every twist of the rack and thumbscrews must be applied with precision. . . . Isaiah, have you done?"

The smuggler stepped back and dropped the curtain into place on his side of the bed. "Done. Our doxy's in luck, as ye may say. Could've gone the way of poor old Jude Maskel. Good man, Jude. Give me safe lodgings, many's the time."

Stephen's sardonic humor was gone. "I know. But our pretty prisoner may know how we can find the gang. And sooner or later, she is certain to tell us."

Growing more and more uncomfortable, Favia watched apprehensively as the smuggler left the room. She had begun to feel that he was more her friend than Stephen Kyle might be. Trying to restore that earlier joking relationship, she teased, "Then, you were serious about applying the rack and thumbscrew?"

He looked at her for a long, uncomfortable minute. "What is your relationship to Peeber?"

Surely he could not doubt her firm answer. "None whatever. I had never seen the creature before. Ugly brute!"

Was she mistaken or did he seem relieved? "Then, how did you find yourself at Jude Maskel's inn, and at that hour?"

"I was on my way to Darking Hill, of course."

That startled him. "To visit—?"

"The Duchess of Hungerford. She stood my friend once, and I hoped that with her new situation here, she might need another abigail. She seems to have full households in each of her estates."

"So you and Her Grace remain friends. I thought you had quarreled. Her Grace seems amply represented by maidservants since she has come to stay in the old squire's house."

That annoyed Favia. So, Beatrix had already visited Stephen, or worse, been visited by him! "She stays for the benefit of the sea air, no doubt."

"No doubt. She told Selina something of the sort at the last assembly. She was very popular. A genuine duchess, you know."

She wanted the sea air. As though the Brighton air were not salty enough!

He showed a magistrate's persistence in pursuing her story. "You were traveling to see the duchess. In what manner?"

"Hibbings, the under-coachman at Dalreagh, offered to drive me there. Then a wheel came loose, and we stopped at the inn. Peeber and his gang were there." She mingled truth with lies in a generous way. "I suspect Hibbings was

127

a member of the gang. They drove off together in my—in the coach."

His fingers drummed on the bedpost as he watched her. "If this Hibbings was one of them, why was it important to take you prisoner? Or, indeed, to carry you into Sussex at all?"

She hesitated, at a loss for an answer, and he reached into his breeches pocket, taking out something and exhibiting it. It was one of the pearl earrings that had belonged to her grandmother, and it gleamed richly in his palm.

She scowled at his carelessness. He must have carried it around in his breeches pocket while he worked out of doors at whatever physical labor country justices of the peace found to do. He might have lost it a hundred times, or dropped it in mud or farm ordure. In a sense, it was an insult to her grandmother.

She reached for it, but he drew his hand back, just beyond her fingertips tantalizingly. "You were carrying this, weren't you?"

"Certainly," she snapped.

"And other jewelry. I stepped on this as I carried you out of the taproom."

"It must have fallen off when you picked me up."

He shook his head. "You were not wearing its mate. I would have noticed. You forget. I had you in my arms for at least an hour as I rode home."

She colored a little at this suggestion of intimacy but managed to argue with spirit, "Surely, even a lady's maid may own pearl earbobs. They may have been a gift." —

His eyes narrowed. "From whom?"

She looked away, saying quietly, "I do not accept gifts from gentlemen, if that is what you imply. It is not at all the thing to do."

Yes. He was relieved. She could not mistake his reaction

128

this time. He did not go so far as to smile, however, and he returned to his original suspicion. "You stole what you call 'earbobs' and took them with you when you left Dalreagh. That is why this coachman-highwayman brought you to Lemuel Peeber, to steal them from you. Those and whatever other little trinkets you took with you."

She hesitated. Perhaps he had provided her with the opportunity to make her true confession. "What would you say if I told you I was Favia Dalreagh, the owner of those jewels?"

He laughed shortly, unpleasantly. "You would not be in this house. Selina would see to that, if I did not."

She waved her hand, gave it a twinge that made her wince, and remarked, "They must have committed no less than murder against your family. I did not know the vendetta was practiced in England."

"The less aid on that subject, the better. My sister is determined to reform 'the little thief,' as she calls you."

"Do you think she will succeed?"

"I doubt it."

To her surprise, he reached over her head, then pinched her nose unromantically, and told her, "Rest now. We will see how you feel about broth and a wine posset later. You are safe here for the moment, but I warn you, if any of the silver is missing, I will personally order you to be tossed into the Channel." He left her before she could decide whether she should end her masquerade and perhaps lose him forever.

It seemed that his smuggler friend was waiting in the hall for him. She heard Stephen call out, "Your patient goes very well. You are an excellent physician, Isaiah."

Then the smuggler: "There's some'ut about that doxy. She's not what she seems."

Favia listened anxiously. She was shamed by Stephen

129

Kyle's reply. "Rubbish. The girl has found life a rough business and learned to take what she can make off with. You can hardly blame her. She has been surrounded by wealth most of her life. Wasted fortunes that were not hers."

"Mighty pretty, sir. Any female that looks pretty in that cap is almighty fine to begin with."

"I hadn't noticed," Stephen said, and they went off together, giving Favia much to think about.

CHAPTER ELEVEN

Somewhat to Favia's surprise, in spite of her headache and the unsettling inquisition by her host, she slept for a time after that visit. When she awoke again, it was close to midday. She felt very much better. Even her headache had faded to a mere wisp of itself, which vanished after a heavyset, sullen woman of middle years, possibly the cook, brought her nourishing beef broth and the promised "wine posset," which seemed to contain an assortment of spices in addition to spirits.

For the rest of the long day she found herself well enough to be bored. When the smuggler, Micklehouse, visited her that evening at dusk and prescribed a meal of battered eggs and some of the local stewed apples, she felt well enough to dine at a table, but Miss Selina agreed with Micklehouse that she must not rise until morning when "we will see to more activity."

Stephen Kyle looked in once, about eight o'clock that night. He was dressed formally in the black and white made mandatory by that fashion-pattern, Beau Brummell, and she wondered what lucky young female he would take in to dinner. He found Favia spirited enough to discuss what he conceived to be her immediate future. "I assume you would prefer to remove from this bed as soon as possible. Some light activity? Would you like that?''

Perhaps a walk with her host, Favia thought. Or a tour of the village. She agreed that some activity was exactly what she needed.

He smiled his satisfaction. ''You are here at just the right time to attend the Staff Ball. On the threshold of summer. It is held every year. The staff of every considerable household in Darking Hill and Rye and Ashforth. All the villages.''

The staff. She hadn't been thinking in terms of ''Libbie Beckett'' 's servitude.

''Unfortunately I fear that would—''

''We must find you a wardrobe of sorts. It will be a great gala. We all attend.''

This changed matters. ''But of course. I would be happy to oblige.''

''Excellent. Now, I need to know several details about the Dalreagh carriage and the team. I remember seeing the team at Dalreagh, but it was evening, and the lantern light flickered badly.'' She noted that he became more business-like, more the magistrate, and she was slightly intimidated.

''The most distinguishing marks about the coach were its age and the fact that it was so very much out of the present mode.

''And the crest on the doors,'' she added with sudden enthusiasm. ''That should be distinctive.''

He did not share her optimism. ''That is the first thing they will have painted out or disguised.''

''So close to the Channel, too,'' she added, downcast. ''It will be easy to go abroad.''

But here he could be more encouraging. ''Not with that coach. Any sailor is likely to remember its cumbersome size and shape. The task of embarking and landing at Ca-

lais or Boulogne would be noted by dozens of witnesses.''
He added matter-of-factly, ''Then, too, Micklehouse has
many friends here and on the French coast. He will have
word at once. As a matter of fact, they may have considerable difficulty until they dispose of the coach. Sell it or
abandon it. So, we've reason to believe we may soon have
them.''

''Why did I ever leave Dalreagh?'' she mused aloud.

His smile reassured her. He said cryptically, ''There may
be reasons you know nothing of. I'll leave you to rest
now.'' He touched her hand lightly, and after wishing her
a casual good night, left her to go to his formal dinner.
She closed her eyes and went to sleep counting upon that
promised ''activity'' with him on the morrow.

Late the next morning, after the maid brought the early
tea—''it's a habit with the mistress,'' she explained—Favia
was ready for the promised ''activity,'' whatever that involved.

Still alone, she spent very little time in bed. She was
curious about her situation, the house itself, and the view
from what proved to be the two east casement windows
that opened to face the distant Channel.

She pushed open one of the windows and looked out.
The sight was breathtaking. The Kyle house appeared to
be perched on a cliff's edge. A narrow footpath ran down
the cliff at a forty-five degree angle, ending in the watery
marshes where a number of dories and a lugger were tied
up between the willows and the cliffside. Several marshy
streams meandered toward the distant English Channel,
over which the usual clouds and patches of fog hovered.

She watched men who appeared to be sailors working
about the little boats and wondered if they were smugglers
unloading their cargoes of spirits from the enemy shores so
close across the Channel. This was one group of citizens

133

for whom the eternal quarrels between France and Great Britain had no meaning. At the moment the two countries were at peace, but this had no bearing on the excise taxes applied by the governments involved, so that the age-old smuggling went on despite the death penalty they faced.

The sight of all this activity reminded Favia of the peculiar moral views exhibited by Stephen Kyle and his sister. Those views, so violently opposed to Favia's own Tory upbringing, seemed a trifle less peculiar since she found herself being treated like a woman of a lower social order. In all her years she could not recall having asked herself what her own life would be if she were not Lady Favia, the daughter of a belted earl, and, on her mother's side, a descendant of the conquering Plantagenets.

Until this morning she had thought of her "Libbie Beckett" identity as no more than a masquerade, but small matters, milestones, along the way, had begun to show her that in some respects she was little more than a chattel. If she really were "Libbie Beckett" and could not obtain a post, what would become of her?

No matter. She was not that odious abigail, and she could transform herself into Favia Dalreagh at any moment she chose. If the Kyles refused to believe her, she could certainly count upon Beatrix Hungerford, who would be only too happy to vouch for her true identity. Remembering Stephen's concern for her, however, and his apparent revulsion toward the Dalreaghs, she made up her mind to avoid Beatrix, at all costs. For the moment.

She turned away from the window determined to win her host's unqualified approval, so much so that when he discovered her true identity his affections would conquer his prejudice. It might take a bit of doing, but Favia had never shied at an obstacle and was, in fact, a bruising rider toward any goal she had chosen.

Holding up the great swathes of material in her nightrail to prevent tripping over the hems in her bare feet, she saw her reflection suddenly in the mirror above the mantel. The sight was shocking. She had never dreamed she could look so absurd. The bonnet that concealed her hair looked like a mobcap with a frill around it. Her eyes looked enormous. Their color had several times been compared to periwinkle flowers. If so, these periwinkles had been battered by ill-favored winds. She looked far from well. Beyond everything else, she looked ridiculous. After her determination of a few minutes ago, this was a decided setdown.

She looked around, hoping to find some of her own clothing, even if it was merely hung upon pegs in the wall. There was a clothespress in the corner on the far side of the bed but this proved to be locked. Heavens! They really did believe she was a thief.

She dragged off the bonnet, shaking the unruly short curls that badly needed combing. This produced a renewal of her headache, and she groaned but paid little more attention to it. She must look at least reasonably human when her host returned.

A large silver-framed portrait at the end of the mantel caught her attention, and she returned to examine the sweetly smiling face of a young woman with a coiffure very much in the present mode, so Favia assumed the likeness had been recently painted. A message had been neatly written across the high, very proper lace neckline: *Dearest Selina and Stephen, we grow ever closer*. It was signed: *Deborah Mortmain*.

Favia was pricked by jealousy. One of those honey-sweet creatures with all the perfections. If that marked Stephen Kyle's taste in females, there was little hope for Favia. Without wanting to, she glanced toward the portrait again. The young woman was undeniably pretty. She seemed to

135

have little vitality or expression except the gentle sweetness of the eyes and the closed lips with their tight smile, but any male must admire Miss Deborah Mortmain.

Favia sighed. Hearing footsteps in the hall, she hurriedly climbed into bed and tried to make herself look more presentable in the seconds that remained. It was not easy.

A young girl in a full-skirted, black uniform with a white fichu scratched on the door, though it was ajar. Favia heard Selina Kyle urge her, "In, girl. In. She won't bite you."

The girl murmured something in a nasal, whining voice, only to have Miss Selina dismiss it. "Nonsense. The girl is a thief, not a cutthroat. You will note that she holds no terrors for me." Offended though she was, Favia almost smiled at that. One could scarcely imagine a thieving abigail who would hold any terrors for Selina Kyle.

The girl shuffled around the room, putting everything Favia had touched back in its original place, though it might be a matter of inches: a chair, the portrait of Deborah Mortmain, even the coverlet on the bed, which she refolded while Miss Selina limped to the bed and looked down at Favia.

"Feeling more yourself, I'll wager."

"Yes, thank you." Recalling her role she added, "Thank you, ma'am."

"Good. You'll soon be right as a trivet."

"Might I have my clothes? I would like to dress. I feel so helpless here in someone's bed—ma'am."

Miss Selina approved. "A good start. Enthusiasm is a great help in the reformation of the human character."

Favia swallowed the insulting implication and attempted a humility that was hardly in her character. "Very true, ma'am. So, if I could have my clothes . . ."

Miss Selina gave a short bark of laughter. "I fear you

136

will never wear that wretched gown again. There are great lengths of the skirt torn away. Even the hem of the silk slip you wore beneath the gown is in tatters.''

Stephen Kyle had seen her in that wretched condition. The thought dismayed her. Obviously the outrage had occurred in her struggle with Libbie Beckett. The girl had coveted her gown as she had coveted the green pelisse and all the clothing in Favia's portmanteaus and bandboxes. They were in Beckett's hands now, with her jewels.

She recovered as rapidly as she could, but it was a nasty shock to relive that horrifying hour at Jude Maskel's inn. Until this minute it had begun to seem like a nightmare. Imagined but unreal. A new idea made her sit up in horror. But what am I to wear?

Miss Selina read her mind and with grim amusement relieved her of one horror. "Not my wardrobe, I assure you, girl. I've better uses for my clothing. However, I may have a few notions. Tabitha Graeme was in service here for some months. Acted as an abigail, parlor maid, seamstress. Gone now, poor soul.''

Uncomfortable over the idea of wearing a dead girl's clothing, Favia asked softly, "How did she—go?''

"With a villainous footman I was redeeming. One of my few failures, if you must know.''

Favia wanted to laugh at her own mistake but luckily refrained.

Half an hour later when the clothespress had been unlocked by the upstairs maid at Miss Selina's order, Favia was less shocked by the idea of wearing the absent maid's wardrobe. There was a uniform, or what seemed to be a uniform, with two fichus, one of pale grass-green and one of lilac, both excellent shades against Favia's spun-gold hair. The costume, with its close-fitted bodice and full skirt,

137

had the effect of exhibiting the slender female form without seeming to do so. An intriguing challenge.

Miss Selina explained that "Libbie Beckett" must not make violent or even hasty moves until the swelling above her brow had been reduced. She was about to leave the room when Favia, with a mingling of curiosity and jealousy, said, "That's a mighty handsome lady in the pretty frame, ma'am."

Selina gave the portrait a critical examination. "A good Christian soul. She and Stephen will probably make a match of it. We've been acquainted with the Mortmains since time out of mind. Brother and sister grew up with Stephen and me. Daniel painted his sister's portrait. He'll never be a Joshua Reynolds. But not a bad attempt, for an amateur."

Favia studied the portrait again. It seemed to her quite as professional as a Joshua Reynolds. A full-length portrait of Favia's father, the fifth Earl of Dalreagh, looked down at all who dined in the Grosvenor Square mansion, now the possession of Cousin Martin, though Favia doubted whether Martin or his new countess really appreciated the scornful look of her father's that the painter had caught so well.

"It looks like an excellent piece of work," she announced, returning to the subject of Daniel Mortmain's portrait of his sister. She forgot her role and added, "It has texture and light that I prefer to Reynolds."

Miss Selina sniffed. "My dear child, don't express yourself on subjects you know nothing about. I assure you, I have seen several Reynolds, and Daniel Mortmain's work lacks the professional touch."

Very satisfactorily set in her place as an unintelligent lady's maid, Favia was surprised and relieved when two brawny females carried up a hip bath and others followed with cans of hot water. It was not the treatment a servant might expect from the mistress of the house, but it succeeded in its purpose. By the time she had bathed and dressed and worked upon her own hair, a task usually accomplished by Beckett or another abigail, she was rather pleased with the results she saw in the mirror.

She went out into the hall, looked up and down, seeing no one, and finally started down a crooked old flight of oaken stairs only to be shouted at from below by an exceedingly tall, frigid male personage in black who proved to be the Kyle butler, Bidlington, a man much more imperious than his master, Stephen Kyle

"Stop! You will henceforth use the back stairs at all times. Kindly recall your place."

"Just what is my place?" she demanded impudently, never dreaming there was an answer. The question had been rhetorical.

"That is to be decided. The matter is in my hands. Report to the housekeeper's parlor. We will discover where you can be of some use. If any."

This sounded ominous. Not at all sure why she permitted such indignities but feeling that only a coward would quit now, Favia obeyed him. What had all this to do with Stephen's talk of "activity"? Unless—she felt a sudden blow of disappointment. Was it her activity in a servant's post that he had referred to?

Losing her way before several closed doors on the ground floor, Favia was found by the man she hoped would extricate her from this servile trap in which she had placed herself. Stephen Kyle, with his tall, straight figure, his burnished hair, and gray eyes, looked so elegant in the neat pantaloons, well-fitted coat, and the snowy white cravat of a gentleman, that he took her breath away.

He had other matters on his mind, which might explain

139

why he waved her toward the housekeeper's room and with the friendly smile of an employer, congratulated her. "You seem to be going on very well, Libbie. Good luck."

Her eagerness at sight of him faded. He had not seen her as a desirable young lady. She was merely one more servant in the household. Remembering pride, she raised her chin and walked into the housekeeper's little parlor as Stephen reached over her head and pushed the door open.

The door closed behind her, and she was alone in the stuffy, old sitting room, facing her true employers. Evidently Miss Selina acted as her own housekeeper, seated at a beautiful old kidney-shaped desk with the butler standing before her, to receive her orders. From the window behind Miss Selina various steep-pitched roofs told Favia that this house was on top of Darking Hill, probably separated from the other half-timbered buildings by a small town square.

Considering her own downcast mood, Favia was glad to see that from this side of the house the sky remained a clear, clean blue. She hoped it might be a sign that things were not as discouraging as they appeared.

Miss Selina looked up. "Ah, here you are, Libbie. Bidlington tells me he may use you in the library. I thought you might be wishing for a bit of exertion after all those hours in bed. You said you felt so well. Just a bit of dusting. Straightening cushions, furniture. That sort of thing." She frowned, staring at Favia. "You are feeling better, are you not? If you aren't, speak up, girl."

"I am in perfect health," Favia said tightly.

"Splendid. Bidlington, you may put Libbie to work. I've dinner matters to discuss with Cook. I devoutly hope that woman hasn't found the keys to the wine cellar again."

Bidlington was emphatic. "Not likely, ma'am. It never

would've happened if I hadn't been sent to Rye on Mister Stephen's business that morning."

"Hmph. That's as may be. Go. I've things to be done. The Mortmains will be here at any moment, and dinner all too soon."

So, that explained Stephen Kyle's finery! Favia went off with the butler, hardly knowing whether to be grateful or humiliated when Miss Selina called after them, "Remember. Nothing of a physical nature for the girl. And, Libbie, if you have the slightest return of that headache, call for help. You understand?"

"Perfectly, ma'am."

"Libbie?"

"Ma'am?"

"You are looking splendidly." It was an effort to smile her thanks.

Favia followed Bidlington down the hall to the library at the north end of the old house. The room was in some disorder but pleasantly so, quite unlike the so-called study occasionally occupied by the fifth Earl of Dalreagh. Its formality made it impossible for anyone else to find comfort between its austere walls.

Bidlington rang for one of the heavy-handed maids, who arrived with a duster and several cloths. After a consideration of the cloths and memories of his instructions from Miss Selina, he left the duster with Favia, ordering her, "The surface only. But there must be no dust when you are done."

"Aye, sir." She almost added "captain" after his retreating form, so much did he remind her of a seaman with the power of life and death, but his final comment at the door silenced even her audacity.

"Everything is inventoried. I advise you to watch yourself." Obviously he knew of her "light-fingered" past!

Favia applied the duster's iridescent feathers to various faintly scarred surfaces, trying to recall the methods used by her own servants, and reflecting that the dust seemed to fly magically from one surface to another.

The headache had not returned, but she found her task discouraging. Half an hour later she decided it was time to climb the ladder against the wall of books and dust those faded leather surfaces. Most of the books sounded dull to Favia, being political treatises and history, but she was surprised by the presence of Mary Wollstonecraft's *Vindication of the Rights of Women* and similar titles of advanced thinking. They reflected a deep interest in subjects that had come to the fore in the aftermath of the French Revolution. Was Stephen Kyle actually a revolutionary?

She had been so interested in the Wollstonecraft book that she dropped the duster. She looked down between the rungs of the ladder at the worn crimson carpet far below, realizing she would have to climb back down and pick up the idiotic and nearly useless duster.

She was already edging downward, foot by foot, when the study door opened and a man and woman entered. She recognized the heart-shaped face of Deborah Mortmain with no difficulty whatever. The thin young man with her, wearing square-rimmed spectacles perched on the bridge of his nose, was very likely her brother, the artist. A curious artist, indeed, if he was half-blind.

"Heavens!" Miss Mortmain exclaimed. "How very dark Stephen keeps it in here. Young woman, have you seen Mr. Stephen in the past few minutes?"

Favia pointed down the hall. "Outside the housekeeper's room. Would you mind handing the duster up to me?" She thought this over a few seconds, aware of their stupefied silence at being ordered about by a parlor maid, and added, "Sir."

"Extraordinary," the lady murmured. "But it is obvious. Stephen is not here. Daniel, give that—object to the young person. Stephen must be frantic, wondering where we are."

The thin young man adjusted his spectacles and peered up at Favia who suggested, "Beneath your boot, sir."

"Er—yes. To be sure." He stooped, felt for the duster, and tried to reach it up to her. It did not quite reach her, and he climbed up a rung, offering the duster. As she took it, thanking him, he pushed his spectacles up higher on his nose and stared up at her. "I say, you there. Have you ever had your likeness painted? You know. On canvas?"

Favia was amused and absurdly enough, flattered. "Well, now, I don't rightly know, sir. That is to say, a gentleman said so once. Made me a deal of promises, he did. But I never saw—seen the thing when he'd done it. If he'd been and done it."

"Daniel, I vow, you would paint a stray feline on the wharves if it so much as crossed your path." The sweet expression remained despite the words. Miss Mortmain patted her brother's shoulder. "Come along, dear. Paint someone more worthy of you. Selina tells me the girl takes things. It seems she had a falling-out with her friends, some gallows birds who prey on travelers. They bound her up and left her where Stephen found her, in that wretched inn. Even so, she had stolen jewels belonging to an earl's daughter."

Daniel Mortmain backed down the ladder, still gazing up at Favia, who disliked his sister on general principles and favored him with a sunny smile. He blinked. Miss Mortmain pinched at his sleeve. "Do come along, Daniel. Leave the young person to her—to whatever she seems to be doing."

She urged her brother out the door. Favia wrinkled her

143

nose after them, reflecting on the idea of that lady's astonishment when she learned Favia's true identity. In spite of that sweet, simpering, righteous look, she certainly did not share the charitable qualities of her friends Stephen and Selina.

Favia flipped the duster over the shelf and the spines of the aging books, but it was an unconscious gesture. She was wondering suddenly if she herself had exhibited such contempt for servants at their work. Certainly not. But perhaps, upon occasion? At least once or twice? Her conscience troubled her.

When the butler, Bidlington, called her shortly afterward, she was forced to admit she had not finished dusting the wall of books. He received this news with eyebrows that told Favia he had expected as much, but he beckoned her ahead of him along the heavily beamed hall, which possessed a chilling dampness even on the verge of summertime. She supposed this must be due to the location, so near the Channel, and those confusing, tangled marshes she had seen from her casement window.

It was humiliating to discover that her "crimes" were to be paraded before the Mortmains, but there they were in a country parlor that evidently served as a salon. Brother and sister were seated side by side on an aging Jacobean couch with their backs to the long windows opening upon a little cobbled square that seemed to be the center of the village. They sat like judges, expressionless, watching and doubtless analyzing her every move.

Favia remembered to curtsy but then looked to Stephen Kyle for help. She could have sworn he was enjoying himself. He stood leaning back negligently against the brickwork of the unlighted fireplace, never taking his eyes off her.

The interrogation did not begin with promise. "We are
144

discussing your problem and your future, Libbie. Have you any suggestions?

"Mr Kyle is good enough to say that he may not press a charge against you for your part in the crime against Jude Maskel," Miss Mortmain informed her obligingly. "You certainly must thank your benefactor for that, I should think."

"Indeed, sir, I do." Favia dipped another curtsy, this time directly to Stephen, holding tight rein on her temper.

Stephen waved away thanks like a generous man who needs no reminder of his good works. However serious his mouth looked, his eyes were amused, but what he said was far from amusing. "How would you like to go to Miss Mortmain as her abigail, Libbie?"

CHAPTER TWELVE

Favia gasped. Her head seemed to be spinning. An awkward silence followed. She broke it with an effort. "Oh, but I couldn't, sir. I'm that thankful, ma'am! I wouldn't have Your Excellency to think I'm not thanking you, but it just wouldn't do."

"I am not 'Your Excellency,' Libbie," that lady reminded her gently. "I wish to oblige your benefactor, and he seems to believe you need a post. Naturally it would be a brief arrangement, dependent upon your conduct, my dear."

"That's the matter of it, ma'am." Favia glanced helplessly at Stephen Kyle. "I'm not real certain I'm a reformed person. Me being that fond of gewgaws and earbobs, and such like."

Miss Mortmain's heart-shaped face was soft and distressed as she, too, tried to enlist Stephen's understanding. "You see, my poor friend? I fear it is too late. The girl is already hardened to crime. What a pity! And so young, too."

Stephen Kyle nodded, tapping his forefinger against his upper lip. "As you say, a great pity. Her former employer, the Duchess of Hungerford, would not do. It is highly likely that the Dalreaghs have confided to her this girl's behavior. Clearly she needs more training. Selina seems to think no one has given her sufficient trust. To counteract the influence of Peeber and his friends.''

Deborah Mortmain inclined her head and reached out to give him the comfort of her touch. "How like you, Stephen! I wish—'' She tried to attract her brother's eye. "Why, Daniel was saying only this morning, how very like you it was to attempt the rescue of a murderer's consort! Daniel?''

But Daniel's thoughts were elsewhere. "Stephen, would it be possible for the young person to pose for me? I should like to attempt reducing that hair and those eyes to canvas.''

Stephen considered Favia who stood before them, contemptuously brushing imaginary dust off her lilac fichu, debating whether to disclose her true identity. He said finally, "It might be a challenge for you, Daniel. Those eyes are a rare shade. However, if you would care to attempt the subject, I am persuaded some enthralled male will purchase it.''

"Really, Stephen,'' Miss Mortmain chided him smilingly, "you must not encourage conceit in the girl. It will only make life more difficult for her when you are forced to remand her.''

"Remand?'' Stephen repeated.

"To wherever she will be incarcerated, of course.''

Favia stiffened. With anger, humiliation, and a strong sense of danger she waited for Stephen's answer. He took this strong hint with a terrifying gravity. "Very true. But we must all do what we may to save her from such a fate. If, that is, she has reformed. What do you say, Libbie?''

Favia said between her teeth, "I'm sure I wouldn't know, sir. May I go now—sir?''

147

"While we decide your fate? Is that wise?"

Out of some wild impulse to annoy both Stephen and Miss Mortmain, she burst out with a fine pretense of enthusiasm, "By the by, Mister Artist, I'd be mightily pleased to make a pose for your canvas thing anytime Your Worship names."

She had succeeded in annoying Miss Mortmain, but the glitter of some emotion remained in Stephen's eyes, and she had made the artist exceedingly happy. He sat forward, pushing his spectacles up on his nose in his nervous gesture. "That would be most kind of you, Miss . . . Libbie. As Stephen says, it would be a true challenge, but I believe I can rise to it."

Favia made her voice as honeyed as possible. "You're a real gentleman, you are, sir. And a great artist. A body can see that with half a glance."

She had won over Daniel Mortmain, whose plain, studious face blushed scarlet with pleasure, but Stephen looked less pleased. His mouth set, and Favia wondered if he could be jealous, an idea that delighted her. He said abruptly, "You may go, Libbie. We will decide later what is best for you and your future."

She dipped a curtsy that was as insolent as she could make it, then turned to leave the room, but she passed the artist on her way out and took care to give him her warmest, most pathetic smile.

The butler had been waiting for her in the chilly hall. In the best of circumstances the man behaved as though he were lord of the manor, and at his worst he was a tyrant to those in his power. It was a situation entirely foreign to Favia, and she found it impossible to conceal her dislike.

He stood directly in her way with both hands clasped behind him and an expression of such disdain that she had a great, if impractical, desire to shake him until his teeth rattled.

"Beckett. That is what you are called?"

"Yes, Your Honor," she agreed, with strict attention to honesty.

"Then, be on your way, and try to recall in future that there will be no loitering in the principal chambers of the house."

"I was called in by Mr. Stephen. To loiter. And as I was dismissed, I was on my way up to my room. Your Worship."

"You will find the service stairs behind you. And I am not Your Worship. I am Bidlington. You may regard me as your immediate superior so long as you are employed here. Now be off."

More annoyed than ever because she had placed herself in the wrong, she swung about and marched to the back stairs. By the time she had reached the lovely room that was temporarily assigned to her, she was in a turmoil of indecision. Was this the moment for unveiling Lady Favia Dalreagh? Stephen Kyle was proving far more class—conscious today than he had in Brighton, or even at Dalreagh? What had come over him?

If she gave up her masquerade, of course, she would lose that disgusting wager with Beatrix Hungerford and Vincent Kinsham. She had counted upon His Highness, the Prince Regent, to forbid the wager when he thought his wife had encouraged it, but that hope seemed to be dashed.

Meanwhile, very soon, her mother would begin to wonder why she had received no message from Favia. The countess seldom noticed anything that did not have a direct influence upon her own comfort. Still, she did not want her mother to worry.

She crossed the room and suddenly became aware of

Deborah Mortmain's portrait, those angelic eyes gazing at her with just a smidgen of self-righteous pleasure.

"You are much too angelic for Stephen Kyle. He spends his life fancying he can change the world. But I have a notion your ambition in life is to change Stephen Kyle. . . . Not for the better, I make no doubt."

The woman continued to regard her with the same complacency, and Favia was forced to turn the portrait around before she could make any further decisions.

She tried to open the clothespress, but it was locked again. So much for the Kyles' trust in thieving "Libbie Beckett."

Climbing up to sit on the side of the bed, she gave her predicament a few minutes of calm thought. She still wanted to make Stephen Kyle aware of her as Favia Dalreagh, but none of her own clothing remained to her. Even her earrings were in Kyle's hands.

Her hands. She looked down at them, studying their smooth shape, the record of her obvious failure to earn her own way in that world that existed beyond the haut ton. At least, she did not display half a dozen rings in the manner of Beatrix Hungerford. One ring. Bright pink gold with a single opalescent pink pearl that had turned on her hand and was hidden from the casual observer. When traveling, she often turned the stones of a ring inside. With so many footpads lurking on the outskirts of London, and many of the roads infested by highwaymen, she did not intend to encourage them.

Today it represented her only financial power. If she were in London, she might take the ring to a respectable jeweler's and receive sufficient money for her purposes. Here in rural Sussex she doubted if anyone would be in a position to buy the ring, or lend her money with the ring as hostage.

She removed the ring with a little difficulty, finally succeeding after she had put it in her mouth and eased it off with her teeth. She examined it, reading the simple engraving that proclaimed the motto of her family: FIDELIS DALREAGH.

Her father had always insisted that the words were juxtaposed and improper, but the motto of her family was too old to quibble with at this juncture. She wondered what procedure was followed in borrowing money, or even selling a reasonably precious jewel. Viscount Kinsham was always talking about "cent-per-cents" and friends of his who borrowed from him rather than face these men.

There might be difficulty, and there certainly would be embarrassment, but it must be done. At any moment, if she wanted to send a message to her mother, or even to the Duchess of Hungerford, her only other acquaintance here, she might find it necessary to bribe someone. She glanced at the silver frame whose portrait now faced the mirror above the mantel. This gave her no satisfaction, but it did remind her of another use for the money the ring would fetch at a jeweler's.

If she remained here under these barbaric conditions she intended to show herself to the best advantage at what Stephen Kyle called "the Staff Ball." She would hardly be content with her present wardrobe of one uniform with only two fichus to brighten it.

She stepped down from the bed, went to the door, and looked out. The hall was deserted. She considered herself, removed that sign of servitude, the stiff little white-muslin tiara, from her hair, and started toward the dark service stairs, feeling like a prisoner escaping from jail. She barely avoided Miss Selina on the ground floor, discussing the servant problem with Deborah Mortmain.

Stepping out into the village square, she startled a young

housemaid who had been looking back over her shoulder, waving at a somewhat chinless youth in the severe Spanish livery of Beatrix Hungerford's Spanish ancestors. Luckily neither the maid nor the chinless boy recognized Favia as one of the duchess's guests in Brighton and London.

Since it was quite possible Beatrix herself might be in the vicinity, Favia made a special effort to avoid being seen by the crowd shuffling past the various village shops, the half-timbered old tavern, and the tiny stone church beside a flight of stone steps leading down to the marshland.

All the cobbled streets plunged steeply downward off the little hill. If Favia followed any of these, the return would take far too long, so she contented herself with investigating the shops around the square. Unfortunately a jeweler's shop was not among them.

She received several glances and whispered comments from various citizens who recognized her position by her costume and buzzed with arguments over the household that employed her. No matter. She was amused but unconcerned.

She had one overriding problem: to find someone who would lend her the money for her ring. On an impulse she entered two shops, one, a mercer, whose elderly female proprietor was berating a scullery maid from the back regions of the shop. The chances of borrowing money here, even on a ring, looked unpromising.

The second proprietor, a male in a coffee house, was deaf and could not understand the transaction she had in mind.

The third and last possibility that occurred to her was the tavern with its noisy custom and an obvious look of prosperity. It wasn't until she had ventured into this half-darkened taproom, which smelled of strong spirits, that she decided it was not the place to transact her business.

She was about to turn back into the narrow entrance passage when she realized that the several deep-throated and alarming voices calling out for "the doxy" were actually summoning her. She did not look around, but from the direction of their voices, they were all either leaning on the tapster's bar or sprawled at a table in front of it, drinking mugs of rum, and the gin that they referred to, with reason, as "Blue Ruin."

"Have a drop or two along of me, there's a good gal!"

"Curse you, Nat! I seen the doxy afore ye. Here's me lap, girl, come coze with Old Sam'l."

The rest were worse. Undoubtedly they were all smugglers, or as near as made no matter.

Deeply conscious of her exposed ankles in this parlor maid's livery, and aware that her identity for once gave her no protection, she tried to retain some shreds of dignity while she increased the speed of her departure. She had just reached out for the timbered door when it was pushed open and a gaunt young man entered, looking curiously blind as the lamplight above the tapster's head was reflected in his spectacles.

She caught at Daniel Mortmain's bony shoulders. "Oh, sir! I'm ever so glad to see you. I have an errand for you from your sister."

It was the first thing she could think of. Luckily he cast a quick look behind her and understood her problem.

"Yes, indeed. Come along. My poor girl, how did you come to visit the tavern? Not a very respectable place for anyone as pretty as you."

She let him take her arm and escort her out to the fresh, wind-washed street, where she took a long breath of relief. The young man, meanwhile, kept a tight grip on her arm. His solicitude was kindly meant but faintly annoying. It

153

suggested helplessness, which she was far from feeling, now that the danger was over.

Returning to essentials, the artist asked the embarrassing question. "Let me see. You say you have a message from Deborah?"

She tried to look demure and apologetic. It was easier after her recent plunge into the male haven of the tavern. "I beg pardon, sir. It was the first thing I saw . . . seen."

"Saw," he corrected her automatically. "I should have realized why you said that." He hesitated upon hearing footsteps on the huge cobbles behind them. She sensed his timidity, and when he said abruptly, "Oh. I thought I heard my sister. She is somewhere in the village," Favia guessed that the real terror of his life was Deborah Mortmain. She of the angelic face.

"Sir, you are a splendid painter. You should go up to London and paint the ladies of the Great World."

He was pleased. "I believe I have some small talent. The portrait of Deborah was exhibited, you know. Have you seen it?"

"Wonderful. Where, sir?"

"In Hastings. Hastings isn't far from Brighton, you know. And His Highness is at Brighton."

"He was at Brighton."

Almost before she said it she knew the remark was a mistake, but he saw nothing strange in her knowledge. "True. I had forgotten. You were in service with the Dalreagh female." He lowered his voice confidentially. "I've heard it said that women like that actually chastise their maids with the backs of their mirrors."

"What?"

"Mirrors or some such weapon. Brutality. Nothing but brutality among our titled rulers."

"Heavens!" It seemed likely that Stephen Kyle was

154

spreading this foul rumor. She had seldom resented anything so much. "Did Mr. Kyle tell you this?"

"Very likely. Told Deborah and, of course, Selina knows. We are most sympathetic to your problem. Libbie. We all know why you were forced to leave the Dalreagh service."

"And I collect that Miss Deborah is also sympathetic."

He said quickly, very defensive, "By all means. She feels as Stephen does, in everything."

"But not in the matter of Libbie Beckett."

She had caught him on that. He looked uncomfortable. "You must not take Deborah's—ah—frankness as a sign of her disapproval. She is simply direct and honest in all things."

Favia hoped the lady was more honest in other matters than she had been in Favia's presence when she had so clearly revealed her dislike of Stephen Kyle's rescued criminals while pretending otherwise.

But this was no way to win the timid artist's favor. She summoned all her acting ability to assure him, "How true, sir! You reassure me." It occurred to her that Stephen Kyle deserved a sharp setdown, and she went on, "I shall try and remember that Master Kyle is merely teasing me when he makes those proposals of—But it is his odd humor. Nothing more. I shall pay him no heed. In any case, he cannot be serious in suggesting that I should become his dependent or face the hangman."

Daniel Mortmain stopped and stared at her. "You cannot mean it. Not Stephen."

She became flustered. "No, no. Certainly not. Do not heed me. These are gentlemen's jesting ways."

"That you should be subject to such treatment, in the fellow's own house!" He considered and came to a solution that horrified her. "It is clear, you must come to Mortmain. As Deborah's abigail.'' He gave her a shyly flirtatious grin. "I give you my word, Libbie, I shall not repeat the liberties of others who should know better."

She hurried to disavow her former hints. "Oh, no, sir. Miss Selina would not permit anything of that sort."

"Still, I do not like to think of a delicate creature like you at the mercy of a bounder."

"Not a bounder, sir. He was only teasing."

"I confess, I never thought Stephen capable of taking advantage in that fashion." Another idea came to him suddenly, a suggestion that better pleased him. "I shall ask that you come to Mortmain while I sketch you."

She wanted to avoid Mortmain, if possible. "Or perhaps you may sketch me at the Kyle house, where I will be near at hand if Miss Selina should need me."

He agreed, his enthusiasm rising.

They were both startled by a well-remembered voice, deep and full for a female, edged with an ominous note of cynical laughter. Beatrix Hungerford.

They swung around on the street together to see the duchess sweep toward them over the time-rounded cobblestones, with a sour-faced abigail and the chinless footman following in her wake. Although the village was too steep and high for horses and wheeled carriages, she managed to stop the not-inconsiderable foot traffic by her awesome appearance. She was a splendid monolith, all in black taffeta, with her thick dark hair only partially covered by an exquisite black-lace mantilla. Lest anyone imagine she was still a widow in mourning, she wore a vivid red rose at the point of her neckline that called upon the eye to note her majestic bosom.

"Your Grace." Daniel Mortmain bowed but could not take his gaze from that expansive bosom. His spectacles

156

slipped to the end of his nose, and he pushed them back, swallowing nervously.

The duchess nodded and gave him her wide-lipped smile. It was impossible for her to ignore a male of any age, but her real interest was concentrated upon Favia, who had bobbed her respectful curtsy. The duchess's sloe eyes narrowed. The smile returned. "It is the Dalreagh maid, is it not?"

"Ay, ma'am, Your Grace." Favia waited in suspense, but from the woman's first reaction it appeared that she was still playing Favia's game, doubtless for reasons of her own.

"I daresay, you found Lady Favia too harsh. One learns to make allowances, however. The poor creature has such a vile temper." Before Favia could make the indignant reply that was on her tongue, she held up one gloved hand. "Would you forgive me, sir? I have a matter to discuss with the girl. About her recent employer."

Daniel Mortmain was disappointed, but he tried to be worldly about it. "Certainly, ma'am. And, Libbie, I should like to sketch you the first minute you are available. Perhaps this evening. Or the morning?" To Favia's surprise, he caught himself and apologized. "No. Sorry. Not this evening. We've no moon. Tomorrow."

A curious remark. What did it mean? Why should he be concerned about the moon, and especially the fact that this was the dark of the moon?

When he had strolled away, the duchess dismissed her own entourage and became confidential. "Ah, at last we can be ourselves. My dear Favia, do tell me. How under heaven can you keep to this unpleasant masquerade? You look perfectly ridiculous, you know. You are not meant by nature to play the soubrette."

There was much in what she said, but Favia defended

herself with forced humor. "I have been persuasive thus far." She smoothed the wrinkled folds of her skirt and caught the duchess studying her thoughtfully.

"Quite true. Favia, tell me, do you recall the terms of our wager? Prinny holds the stakes. I speak figuratively, you understand. But the stakes themselves finally topped six thousand guineas. It would be difficult to cry off now, with Prinny so closely involved. If your present masquerade is beginning to bore you, you may—*delope*, so to speak. Fire into the air. Surrender. If you cry off, I am willing to settle for half the sum and say nothing to our mutual victim. What do you say?"

There was no hope now that the wager could be canceled. The business had gone too far. To save face, Favia said coolly, "I never cry off."

"And when that delightful Master Stephen discovers that you have made him the fool in your little masque?"

"Are you going to tell him?" She asked it calmly, but her heart was beating fast.

The duchess considered her fingers, one finger at a time, massaging the glove. "I give you my word, I shall not do that." She laughed abruptly, and when Favia was puzzled, she explained with her deep chuckle, "I wonder what you would think, my dear Favia, if you wished to disclose your true identity and then recalled that I had given my word not to say you are Lady Favia. A conundrum, don't you agree?" She shook her finger in Favia's face. "My word is my life and my honor. That is the legend of my family. So, you may rest easily. I shall not betray you. Is there another way in which I may oblige? And perhaps win six thousand guineas? Or will you surrender today and lose only half that amount?"

It would be difficult to pay even three thousand. No matter. Favia owed Stephen Kyle a little humiliation after the stories he had spread about her. Slapping abigails with mirrors, indeed!

"Thank you, no. Let my real identity remain a surprise for that splendid, public-minded Member of Parliament."

"Really?" The duchess definitely looked relieved, for some reason. "I had supposed you and Stephen were going on exceedingly well. But then, I would not know. I haven't seen him since last evening when he came to the manor for piquet and a late supper."

Favia had seen him looking especially handsome last evening when he was about to leave for an engagement. She knew now with whom the engagement was made. And piquet was a game for two players.

The duchess gestured for the footman and maid to join her, then added in the most casual manner, "By the by, my dear, your recent—shall we call them your business partners?—have been seen in the neighborhood by a pair of smugglers. Stephen is on their trail."

"Thank heaven for that," Favia told her coolly.

"Oh, yes. I agree. But gossip does say that Captain Peeber had a female partner with him when he murdered that poor innkeeper. Evidently, this female chose the wise course and separated from him, carrying a pretty collection of jewels. At least, that is the gossip. . . . Something to think about after they capture Peeber, my dear 'Libbie.' "

"Nothing would please me more than the capture of the creature with my jewels."

The duchess smiled. "Of course."

Favia waited until the woman was gone before she shivered. Around her the village at sunset took on a bright, burning glow that contrasted violently with the shadows on the west side of the square. Favia looked around the square, noting for the first time the little shop belonging to a seamstress on one of the steep, cobbled streets wandering down

159

the western slope of the hill. The sunset lights gleamed on the swinging sign: MADAME DUREAU—FRENCH SEAMSTRESS.

The very place. She would try her luck with her pearl ring. Favia walked rapidly down the hill, lowered the brass latch, and went into the shadowed interior. A wedding gown, faintly yellowed by the sun, was displayed across three wooden steps in the little bow window. The gown was made in the style popularized by the Empress Josephine, with the straight, single skirt, the high waistline, and small puffed sleeves. Only the gloves and tiara were missing. The train was draped behind the gown, bordered in royal purple velvet, sewn with golden bees, that very obvious symbol of England's great enemy, the Emperor Napoleon. No one seemed to object. Even now, two women on the street were pointing it out, evidently admiring it.

Across the three wooden counters in the small, airless room were spread sumptuous lengths of silk and popular muslin goods. Displayed on one length of evening gauze was a necklace of garnets, the sight of which encouraged Favia. The owner did sell jewelry.

A small, stout woman in an old-fashioned, pumpkin-shaped wig popped into the room through the doorway behind the rear counter. "Dearie, you'll be wanting Mrs. Nicholson's gown, I daresay. I've just this instant finished it. And a fine piece of work, if I do say so." Her skills might be French, but her voice was unquestionably homespun.

Favia cut her off hurriedly. "No, ma'am. I wonder if you have ever done work and been paid in kind."

"In kind?" The chubby little woman looked sharper.

Favia removed the ring and laid it on the polished wooden surface of the counter. A streak of sunset light caught the pearl and made it glow. The little woman's eyes bulged, but she did not touch the ring.

"How did you come by such an object?"

"It was given to me by my former mistress. I recently left her service. She was returning to her home in Wiltshire." She manufactured a story rapidly. "Her betrothed said it did not suit her. He felt the color in the pearl was not flattering to her complexion."

"It suits you very well, miss." The seamstress' voice was dry. She reached for the ring, considered it, and polished it on her sleeve in a businesslike way. "However, we might strike a bargain." She slipped it on her little finger, where it glowed richly.

A shadow crossed the bow window and then the street door opened. Madame Dureau beamed. "Ah, Master Stephen. How may I serve you? Some trinket for dear Miss Selina?"

Favia was so angry, and so worried by his presence, that she snapped, "It would seem that the entire village is abroad this afternoon. Is no one busy at home in his own lodgings?"

Stephen Kyle laughed, quite a pleasant laugh, in the circumstances. He did not sound angry or suspicious. "Perhaps that is because we knew our pretty Beckett was wandering abroad, and up to no good."

"More likely, you are all spying on me."

Even that did not ruffle him. Fortunately the seamstress had turned her palm up, with the pearl concealed, as she reached under the counter for various trinkets to better display them before his eyes. Favia could only pray that he had never noticed the ring on her own hand.

CHAPTER THIRTEEN

"If we may confine ourselves to business," Stephen suggested with gentle reasonableness. "Some little piece of jewelry for my sister, Selina. What do you have?"

"A brooch, sir?" Madame Dureau brought out a pair and set them before him on the background of a length of white satin.

He said, "Come here, Libbie. Which do you think Selina will prefer? The blue enamel, or the little silver wreath?"

Nervous but determined to carry through the deception, Favia chose the blue-enamel arrow, somewhat puzzled over his indifference to her previous dealings with the seamstress. It was not until Madame Dureau presented him with the little packet that he looked at the woman's hand. Mrs. Dureau clenched it into a fist and tried to hide it behind the counter.

"A rheumatic problem?" he asked sympathetically.

The little woman was unflustered. "Something of the sort. So kind of you, sir." She ushered him and a confused Favia out of the shop.

Favia was asking herself: Can I trust her? Will she steal the ring? Why hasn't he asked me any questions? It was all very frustrating. And if the truth were told, nerve-racking as well.

Stephen, who had appeared to be thinking of matters far removed from the problems of an unemployed abigail, suddenly spoke to her as they approached the two-story stone Kyle house on the east side of the square. "Would it annoy you to pose for Daniel Mortmain?"

"Not at all. Such a very gentlemanlike young man, I always say."

He gazed at her mouth for a long moment. She moistened her lips. Then, to her chagrin, he pinched her chin. "Are all abigails so tantalizing? You expect me to kiss you, and yet, you must know, I am very likely to hang your friend, Lemuel Peeber."

"Good."

"And all who took part in the murder of Jude Maskel."

Breathing fast, she assured him, "I had no part in that. I was a prisoner myself. No one should know better than you."

"You have nothing more to say?"

She was puzzled by the unexpectedly serious note in his voice, and his stern expression. "No, sir. Nothing that—I mean, I've nothing to say."

Binglington opened the door to them. "Miss Selina has asked me to inform you, sir: Dinner will be served promptly within the hour. With Kittering gone to have her tooth drawn, we may use Beckett to help serve, if you think it suitable, sir."

While Favia waited indignantly, Stephen pretended to give the matter some thought. She was sure he intended to use her from the instant Bidlington mentioned the matter. "Eminently suitable. Libbie, how is your head?"

She had forgotten the swelling above her temple, and since he had seen her walking all over the village with no difficulty whatever, she could not plead illness now. "I am quite recovered, sir."

"Very well. Go to your room and wash off the dust of the village. Order up a pitcher of water. Make yourself presentable, and then join the staff in the kitchen or the stillroom."

Bidlington started to elbow her along, but she reminded Stephen, "I have never served at table before. I am an abigail. Sir."

Stephen said, "Bidlington, you had best warn the kitchen that we have a new second maid for the evening."

To Favia's surprise, he took her wrist, preventing her from following the butler. She scarcely knew how to read the intent look in his eyes. She felt excitement, but was also aware of apprehension. After his previous indifference to her, his blatant attempts to demean her in every way, she was unprepared when he cupped her chin in his free hand and bent his head to kiss her.

Despite her careful upbringing, the rigid instructions as to propriety, she was no stranger to kisses. But most admirers had been hesitant, timid, not sure of the promise they thought they had read on her smiling lips when she teased them. If too much passion was shown, or a possessiveness beyond her personal desires, she invariably ended the matter with a cool setdown. Few clumsy admirers were proof against that.

Stephen Kyle, however, gave her no time to demonstrate her control of the embrace. His lips brushed hers in a titillating way that made her shiver pleasurably. When she would have broken away to taunt him or play the shocked maiden, his hand held the lower half of her face in a vise and his mouth captured hers again. She responded with a passion she had never known before, and for a few seconds she was happier than she had ever been.

164

He released her with a little push and the reminder "Hurry along. You don't want to anger Bidlington. He can be quite terrifying, or so the maids tell me."

Waving her arms in a wild gesture of unsatisfied rage, she ran up the stairs. The front stairs. She could not move fast enough, however, to avoid his easy laughter that followed her retreat.

The maids told him! After equally passionate embraces, no doubt. He had taken advantage of her servile position to humiliate her. The power of men in his position over women in hers was shocking. His great crime lay in his success. He had made her desire his caresses and then treated her like the kitchen maid he had made of her. Something must be done. She wasn't at all sure what form that revenge might take, but she would not let this trick pass without paying him in kind.

She arrived in the stillroom in what she considered exemplary time, which was fortunate, in view of the contradictory instructions that both Bidlington and the perspiring female cook bestowed upon her. She was to follow Bidlington, to heed each of the signals he gave her by finger or by a slight inclination of the head. The cook insisted that her duties were to replace the many dishes of the first course and then to take notice of personal tastes during the entire second course.

To both these formidable beings Favia nodded, agreed, and made up her mind to show the world, and especially herself, that she was fully as useful as any other kitchen wench.

There were two added guests in the long, heavily-beamed dining room, an elderly judge and his wife, a tiny creature whose whisper of a voice managed to subdue her blustering husband whenever he started to relate a salacious story.

Deborah Mortmain looked angelically correct in white

165

muslin with a silver-worked shawl draped carefully over her arms. She was attentive to every word spoken by Stephen, so much that she scarcely touched the chicken or the sole, the mushrooms, the *choux-fleur*, or any of the other delicacies that seemed, to Favia, much superior to the imitation French cuisine at Dalreagh.

Miss Mortmain's brother had an appetite, but he seemed to lose it when he saw Favia puttering about in the shadow of the redoubtable Bidlington. She smiled at him over the butler's shoulder, making him blush. In his nervousness he dropped his spoon. She stooped to pick it up and replaced it with a clean spoon handed to her by Bidlington.

When young Mortmain thanked her, she caught the eye, or eyebrows, of Miss Mortmain. Favia avoided her, only to meet the thoughtful observation of Miss Selina. That lady stared at her until she scurried away, angry that she had been intimidated. Should she have ignored the young artist entirely? It was difficult to know which way to turn.

Of one thing she could have no doubt. Stephen Kyle was far more interested in his guest, Miss Mortmain, than in a kitchen maid. Turning to Deborah, he went into considerable detail in relating an episode of his friend Isaiah Micklehouse's life.

Favia was no longer surprised that a justice of the peace should joke with an august-looking judge about the career of a smuggler. It was Miss Mortmain who complained as Favia would have done. "Dear Stephen, remember your audience. Judge Reade will be shocked. One would think we are all savages here on the coast. Smugglers, indeed. Daniel was saying only this morning that we must not regard these criminals in such a light and humorous manner."

Everyone looked at Daniel who had choked on a morsel of fish. The judge winked at Stephen in an obvious conspiracy. Daniel recovered quickly but, as Favia observed, Stephen found something amusing in the little episode. She began to suspect that Miss Mortmain was not privy to all her brother's secrets.

Was this why Daniel had made that odd remark earlier, about the dark of the moon? The artist, with his spectacles and his ingratiating innocence, might be a smuggler. Certainly the idea did not seem to trouble Judge Reade.

The idea of Daniel Mortmain as a criminal intrigued, even while it shocked Favia. Nothing in her life had gone in the normal way since she had left Brighton accompanied by only that treacherous abigail and an under-coachman who'd played her false as well.

She was greatly relieved when she returned to the kitchen for the last time and was dismissed from this particular purgatory with only the invitation to eat what she liked of the veal and the less popular vegetables. It was the first time in her life that she had eaten "remains." She satisfied her hunger hurriedly, fearing that if she stayed longer, she would be assigned to some other task.

She started up to her bedchamber with a new fear. When would they remove her from that comfortable room and place her in some basement cubicle? For the first time in her life also she was asking herself how kitchen servants endured the much-worse conditions in London. I must announce my real identity, she told herself once more.

She reached the pleasant seclusion of her room without hindrance and washed in the now-cold water remaining in the pitcher. A clean comb and a silver-backed brush lay on the mantel beside a flacon of Otto of Roses perfume, a scent she had always found much too sweet. But she appreciated the gesture on someone's part. Judging by the perfume, it had probably been Miss Selina's idea. She rubbed a drop onto her wrist and began to rearrange her hair, piling the curls high in their correct style.

The result was a curious mélange. From the throat down she might easily be a parlor maid, but her head was unmistakably that of a lady of fashion. No matter. The result gave her more confidence, even though it was for nothing more than a night in bed, alone.

She found the clothespress still locked. "Against my thieving fingers," she admitted with cynical amusement. Less amusing was the sight of the ghastly night robe, large enough for two, and the ridiculous, frilled bonnet. Her own morocco slippers, carefully polished before she stepped into them this morning, had become a trifle scuffed, and certainly dusty, after her walk to Madame Dureau's this afternoon, but they must serve her until she regained her own identity or made an arrangement with the little seamstress to borrow money on her ring.

There was always the likelihood that Madame would pretend she had not received the ring, in which case Favia was determined to make a great scene, accusing her of having stolen it. Surely Stephen would defend her in such a case. He knew better than anyone that "Libbie Beckett" had been in service to the Dalreaghs. There was no direct evidence that Libbie had stolen the ring.

Well, she thought at last, not entirely convinced, at the worst, they will send to Dalreagh for the true story. At which time, I must come forward as myself. And lose Stephen Kyle forever.

She shrugged, gave up the complicated tangle, and reached for the petit-point bellpull. The maid hadn't yet closed the heavy green-velvet drapes. She withdrew her hand, remembering almost too late that a servant in her position would be expected to draw her own drapes. In the extraordinary circumstances that she had drapes, or even windows.

She had already crossed the room when Miss Selina scratched on the door and followed this by limping into the room, punctuating her entry by the firm *tap-tap* of her cane.

"Beckett? Come here."

Am I being asked to act as tiring maid? Favia wondered. "Aye, ma'am?" Belatedly she remembered to curtsy.

Miss Selina was looking stern and unbending. She jammed her cane down on the bare, polished boards of the floor. "Do you know what this is about? Speak up, girl. No evasions."

"Evasions, ma'am?" Bewildered, Favia shook her head. Had the woman discovered her real identity? She began hesitantly, "Is it about my name?"

"Your name? Lord love you, no. Come with me."

"Was it the ring? I left it with the seamstress?"

"What ring? Don't evade the subject. We are not discussing rings at this time."

Puzzled and uneasy, Favia did as she was ordered. Her only moment of triumph came when they walked down the front staircase together just as Bidlington appeared in the lower hall. He saw Favia first. "You there, girl. I thought I made the matter quite clear—" His expression changed ludicrously when he saw Miss Selina move out of the shadows beside Favia, into the light of the lamp on the newel post below.

"Run along, Bidlington," that lady ordered him crisply. His curiosity almost overcame his training, but he bowed, turned on his heel, and vanished into the nether regions of the servants' quarters.

Miss Selina grunted. "I devoutly trust that this matter need not reach the other servants. We must settle it at once, and I advise you to cooperate, for your own sake."

169

More and more mystified, Favia agreed. "Yes, ma'am. Like you say, ma'am."

Miss Selina raised her cane and struck the ivory head sharply on one of the dining room doors. To Favia's surprise, Stephen opened the door. He was scowling, clearly in no pleasant mood. "Selina? What is this all about? Deborah is being damnably secretive, and Mrs. Reade will say nothing, but she looks highly interested. What have you women been concocting?"

Miss Selina sniffed. "I wanted this matter to remain among the females. Do go away, Stephen. Join the judge and Daniel among your precious smuggler friends. And don't forget to order in a few bottles of that fine old Madeira for me. I take it, we may also expect new cargoes of brandy tonight."

"Really, Selina," Miss Mortmain objected. "Daniel has no part in such criminal activities. He has gone to join some friends at the inn."

"If you think that," Miss Selina told her, "you are a bigger fool than I gave you credit for."

Favia wished they would come to the subject of this meeting. It was sure to be unpleasant.

Stephen turned to the other women. He had been out of doors, probably with his smuggling friends. His greatcoat still hung loose over his shoulders. His light-bronze hair was ruffled by the wind. Favia did not find him less attractive, for all his informality. Quite the contrary. Forgetting her role again, she demanded, "Will someone please be good enough to tell me why I am here?"

Everyone looked at her, the women with shocked disapproval. She was only interested in Stephen's reaction. He agreed with her. "The girl—er—Libbie is quite right. Speak up, one of you. What has happened?"

Miss Selina sighed. "What a tiresome creature you are,

170

Stephen! It is the enamel brooch you gave me before dinner. A stupid waste of your hard-earned money, but we will say no more on that head."

"Oh, my dear," the judge's little wife whispered. "What a cruel thing to say! And dear Stephen, always so generous, such a good brother."

"A foolish fellow, and well he knows it."

But Stephen was apparently used to his sister's brusque ingratitude. He moved to more critical matters. "What of this enamel brooch?" For the first time he stared at his sister and at the high neckline of her old-fashioned silk round gown. "Where is it?"

"Gone," Deborah announced in a troubled voice. "Simply gone. The clasp was loose, didn't you say, dear Selina?"

Impatient of all this high drama, Stephen said, "Obviously. So, it has dropped off. If you've lost it, I will be happy to buy you another, Selina."

Favia knew at last why these hostile females had brought her here. Her first reaction was anger, but then a curious thing happened. She found herself trembling, as though she were actually guilty of stealing the trinket.

Trying to conceal this alarming sensation, she opened her mouth to speak, but Stephen seemed to have appointed himself her counsel. "Certainly, no one in the dining room took it. If you lost it at the table, then let us look for it. It cannot have gone far." He reached down, turned up the end of the faded rug under the long oak table, then peered under the table itself.

Miss Mortmain was reproachful. "Can you think we have not searched? Stephen . . . Stephen . . . could you believe us so callous, so unfeeling, as to make accusations without proof? We are not inhuman. We admire your charitable intentions, yours and Selina's, but to be rewarded so cruelly—"

"Indeed," Mrs. Reade added her vote. "Miss Mortmain felt it her duty to tell us about the recent crimes of the young person you have employed in the dining room. But we gave her every benefit of a just search before we made our suspicions known to one another. We searched the room at once when Miss Mortmain noticed that Miss Selina was no longer wearing the brooch."

Stephen said roughly, "When did you notice it last?"

Deborah forestalled Miss Selina. "While we dined. I recall how charming I thought it; such an excellent example of your taste, Stephen. That was just before the girl distracted my brother, and he dropped his spoon. If you recall, Daniel was seated to Selina's left."

The judge's wife nodded. Her gray corkscrew curls lent emphasis to her own evidence as they bounced beneath her frilled little lace cap.

"And the girl picked up Mr. Mortmain's spoon. We all saw that."

Favia looked directly into Miss Selina's eyes. The woman's expression was enigmatic. It was hard to know whether she believed the denial or not when Favia said, "I swear to you, ma'am, I did not take your brooch. It would have been absurd. I have no need for such trinkets." Her confident manner and especially her final words further alienated the other two women.

The judge's wife gave out a rude laugh. "Hoity-toity, they take airs these days! Selina, I should certainly call that impudence of the highest order. The judge must hear the matter himself. He has a way of getting the truth from such creatures."

"This is not the judge's affair," Stephen snapped. "You

172

will all help matters by leaving this room. I will attend to the matter myself."

They looked at one another. The two visitors were confused and wondering if they had been affronted. Miss Selina said, "Very true. The Small Salon, ladies. Stephen, try and keep this from the servants. It will only breed gossip of the worst sort."

Not sure of what her own role might be, Favia lingered, expecting Miss Selina would insist that she follow, or, very possibly, Stephen would ask her to stay. She wanted to stay and, she was sure, find the fallen brooch.

When the other women had gone, Stephen removed each of the ladder-back chairs and looked under them. Without glancing at Favia he ordered her, "Stand out of the way. Over by the windows."

"I should very much like to help you. We must find it."

"If you were anywhere near this area, it would be thought that you had replaced it when you were discovered."

"Oh." She hadn't thought of that.

He completed his fruitless search and straightened up, replacing each chair. As he set the last chair in its place, he backed against the sideboard. An elaborate glass epergne, shaped like an elephant with a howdah, shivered at the nudge of his elbow, and he turned to be sure it was unhurt.

Favia heard his muffled exclamation and started toward him. "What happened? Is it broken?"

"Nothing like that." He showed her his hand. In his palm was the blue-enamel brooch.

Her relief was somewhat dampened by her resentment at the humiliation to which she had been subjected. "How did it get there, may I ask?"

"Someone found it, picked it up, I should imagine, and

left it here. Why he, or she, told no one, I've no idea."

He considered the chairs. "Wasn't this Daniel's chair?"

"Beside Miss Selina's. Yes."

He shrugged. "There is our explanation."

Another unpleasant idea occurred to her. "They will say I placed it there while you were searching the floor."

This time he smiled. "Oh, no. I can certainly swear you were not near the sideboard at any time during my search." He reached for her hand, which seemed to have no will of its own. It lay in his for a delicious few seconds before she withdrew it.

"Please, sir, if you would tell those females—I mean, the ladies—that I am not guilty, I would be most grateful."

His smile held a grim edge. "I'll do that, believe me. And afterward there will be a little talk with Daniel. Or Judge Reade. One of them was criminally careless. He should have told Selina he had found it."

"Indeed, sir."

She watched him go down the hall to the Small Salon, a delicate, formal room all in green and gold, which seemed to be used extensively as a ladies' withdrawing parlor while the gentlemen drank their after-dinner port. Near the kitchen quarters someone had left ajar a heavily reinforced door that opened out upon the steps descending to the marshes. Probably Stephen had done so when he returned from his dealings with the smugglers.

She tried to push the door closed. It required effort. At the same time she heard Daniel Mortmain's voice out in the night as he shouted to someone in a dory below. "No, no. Those to the judge. The rest to Mortmain House. The cask on the beach remains here."

His thin, nervous voice reminded Favia of her recent humiliation. She went out onto the top step and started down, alarming Daniel Mortmain, who almost trod upon her foot as he turned around.

"Beckett! What the deuce? You shouldn't be here, you know."

There was no moon, but the stars were out in a curious foggy nimbus that illuminated the scene below and to her right where the marshes shrank away, leaving a narrow, rocky little beach. Several men were unloading casks and bottles while another pair heaved laden bags into a long-boat. No doubt this was the wool being carried to the Continent for trading.

Favia's voice sounded autocratic and arrogant even to herself. "Why didn't you tell anyone you had found Miss Kyle's brooch? What were you thinking of? Did you want it to be stolen?"

"Stolen? But I did—I mean I tried— They were gabble-gabbling so fast, Deborah and Mrs. Reade, even Selina, that they ignored me. I said, 'Did one of you ladies lose this?' And Deborah said, 'Hush. You are interrupting.' Then I said, 'Well, here it is,' and I left it in plain sight beside that glass elephant. You see, the gardener came to say the boats were here, and I was busy."

The explanation sounded logical. She was embarrassed by her own vehemence.

"Thank you, sir." She was about to go back up the steps when she heard a great crash and the screech of torn wood on the rocky beach. This was followed by cursing that shocked Daniel Mortmain more than it shocked Favia, who had often heard worse from her father's grooms at Dalreagh.

The artist clattered down the steps. "Quiet, lads. There's a female here. Whose cask was lost?"

"Looks like Mister Stephen's," Isaiah Micklehouse called to him. "Damned clumsy Frenchie! Lost his hold."

The small, spry Frenchman objected in his own language and laid the blame upon his companion. It was then that the Frenchman's companion looked up.

He and Favia stared at each other for a long, pregnant moment. The chill that engulfed her flesh was only due in part to the night and the lowering fog. She knew that hard, rough face and associated it with the worst hours of her life. He was the seaman called "Bucko," who had been one of Lemuel Peeber's cutthroats.

The man's gaze was steady, but she could well understand the tension that must grip him.

"Is he a new member of your smuggling band?" she asked Daniel Mortmain. He stared at Bucko in surprise. "Yes. First trip. Good seaman, though."

He had been the only one to help Favia that night. And now he must have left Peeber's band.

Favia said nothing more. She went back up the steps and into the house. She wondered what "Bucko" was thinking. She hoped she would never be sorry she had not betrayed him to the hangman.

CHAPTER FOURTEEN

It was Judge Reade who reached out one pudgy hand to caress Favia's fingers and in gentle tones suggested that his wife make the apology that was due to this "unfortunate and vilified young woman." However gentle he might sound, Favia suspected as she withdrew her fingers that he was probably a tyrant on his own estate.

At all events, Mrs. Reade's whispered apology followed.

Favia accepted Mrs. Reade's stiff apology for what it was worth. The woman had been on the verge of brushing aside the entire matter with the vague remark that "one might be pardoned for thinking the worst of servants whose insolence knew no bounds." This aroused Stephen to one of his cold, imperious remarks about "the inhumanity of females who knew the world too little," which his fellow members in Parliament had heard before.

Deborah Mortmain was more amenable and certainly more voluble.

"Dear Stephen, of course, I regret my part in it. A beastly business. I assure you, the evidence was so particular, I found myself making false conclusions in spite of myself. It was hastily done and I, for one, deplore it. I trust you will believe, Stephen, it was never my intention to behave with so little consideration. Forgive me, please.''

"It would have been more appropriate if you addressed Libbie Beckett," Stephen said.

Miss Mortmain flushed at his reminder but dutifully addressed Favia. "You heard my apology, Beckett? Good. Now I must scold Daniel. He produced this appalling fuss."

Miss Selina added nothing to these forced apologies, even when her brother gave her a sharp look. "Come along, Libbie," she said. "I took you from your room. I can at least accompany you back."

By this time Favia was sickened by all these false expressions of regret and glad to go with the brusque Selina.

Stephen opened the door for the two women. They went out without looking at him. Favia was moderately grateful for his efforts on her behalf, but the tensions of the evening, the accusations, the sight of "Bucko," and the day itself finally reached her. She could not remember when she had been so tired and unsure of her own future actions.

With her cane Miss Selina pushed open the door of the room she had given to Favia. Suddenly she broke the silence between them. "I refuse to add mine to their mealymouthed apologies. Nor do I expect you to believe me when I say I hardly thought you were guilty. However, there was always the chance."

"I understand."

"It was fortunate we found the thing so soon. I think you will enjoy the Staff Ball on Thursday."

"I'm sure I will. Good night, ma'am."

Thursday night. Forty-eight more hours. Could she continue her masquerade that long?

Favia bolted the door after the woman. She removed her

uniform and petticoat, got into the huge night robe, dropped the bonnet over the side of the high bed into limbo, and went to sleep. She was tired in every bone and muscle.

It was in the early hours of the morning that she awoke to make decisions, the most crucial being the question of disclosing her true identity after the Staff Ball. But she still hoped to win Stephen's love by looking her best on Thursday night. Small wonder that he regarded her with more compassion than excitement. He had never seen her as anything but a serving woman. As a gentleman with a long lineage, he could never consider marriage to an abigail.

"And it isn't fair. I've worked twice as hard being Libbie Beckett as I ever worked when I was Lady Favia Dalreagh. If my own worth were considered rather than my ancestors, would anyone look at me twice?" It gave her a curious ambivalence about herself, and a newly aroused sympathy for the half of her that had become Libbie Beckett.

She was made even less comfortable the next morning when she was summoned to the housekeeper's parlor and heard names discussed that brought back the vivid horrors of the evening at Jude Maskel's inn.

Miss Selina was asking Bidlington, "How do they know it is this Captain Peeber?"

"Overheard, ma'am. This Peeber was heard over a mug of gin at a Dover tavern. Seems his wench had taken to her heels with the swag, as they call it. Rings and earbobs and some mighty fine stones she'd taken from her mistress."

Favia held her breath.

Selina asked, "Was he alone?"

"A boy and an old man were readying to quit him. They separated from him when the three left the tavern. The

179

tapster heard them claim this Peeber held back their shares. Mad as fire, this Peeber was. Said he'd find the hellion female who'd actually taken them, if his life depended on it. The tapster was cow-hearted and failed to report them until they were gone.''

Favia felt as anxious as if she were Libbie Beckett in very truth. She took a great breath of relief when no one mentioned the name of the ''wench'' who had outwitted Lemuel Peeber and made off with the Dalreagh jewels. Thus far, the hue and cry over Favia Dalreagh had not begun. Evidently her mother believed she was at Brighton, and her Brighton friends imagined she had returned home.

By Friday morning, she thought, all will be explained for good or ill, and I shall have lost the wager. It would mean selling all her important jewelry, but this had begun to fade in importance compared with the loss of the man she loved.

Miss Selina looked up to see Favia standing obediently in front of the kidney-shaped desk, awaiting her tasks for the day.

''Ah. Glad to see you up and about, girl. What with Kittering still the worse for her visit to that tooth-drawing butcher, Bidlington is short of hand in the dining room. However, we will see where we are at dinnertime this afternoon. Meanwhile suppose you complete the dusting in my brother's study and in the Small Salon.''

Favia bobbed respectfully. ''Yes, ma'am. I mean, aye, ma'am.''

''You were correct the first time,'' her employer remarked dryly.

Favia bit her lip but went away at Bidlington's direction. She was dying of curiosity, so she tried her wiles upon the haughty butler. ''Sir, I don't believe there is anyone who knows the important matters the way you do.''

He remained rigid but with a complacent touch. "Doubtless you are correct."

"And that dreadful highwayman, Peeber. Was he captured in Dover?"

"Not yet, but the likelihood is imminent. I collect that the tapster did not report the conversation until the rogues left the tavern. But Master Stephen's men will soon have this Peeber under the hatches."

Favia did not know whether to be relieved or resentful. She never wanted to have anything to do with Lemuel Peeber again. But she also wanted him punished.

"Could Captain Peeber have gotten a boat and gone abroad?" She thought of Bucko working almost under her nose. Peeber, too, might be somewhere along the Romney Marshes.

Bidlington scoffed at such ignorance. "What? With Master Stephen's men everywhere up and down the coast, and this Micklehouse, to boot? Best leave such matters to them that deal in crime and gallows bait. Master Stephen is off to Dover. He'll be talking with the tapster. But your business is here. In this room." He threw open the library door.

Nothing had been done here since yesterday, and Favia went to work vigorously with the feather duster. At the same time her hands shook a little. She was beginning to wonder what Peeber would tell Stephen about that night at Jude Maskel's inn. Would he actually confess that he had bound and gagged Lady Favia Dalreagh? In which case, Stephen must learn the truth about her in the worst possible way.

This time she was allowed to finish dusting before she was interrupted. Miss Selina came in late in the morning and stood leaning on her cane while she ordered the surprised Favia, "Run along to see Madame Dureau about

181

your gown for tomorrow night. She's the best. I've a feeling she will present you with something admirable."

Favia hesitated, supposing the woman would expect her to mention the fact that she had no money. If not, it must mean that Stephen knew about the ring and had told his sister that "our newest abigail can afford a dress. She needs no charity."

Miss Selina looked as if she read Favia's thoughts, but when she spoke it was evident that she knew nothing about the ring. "Mention this house, and tell her it is my order."

She raised her cane, blew lightly on the ivory, and polished it with her left palm. "But that may sound a little imperious." She grinned in a likable way that made Favia think of her brother. "One grows into the habit when encouraged."

"I know." Favia knew very well. Only her experience as Libbie Beckett had shaken that self-assurance.

"Well, then, she is sure to have something she can alter to your figure."

"Gowns ready to hand, that would be something uncommon, ma'am."

"Not new, of course. But clean and adequate. With your complexion and form, you should do very well. Run along now."

Favia ran along. She was anxious to settle with Madame Dureau about her ring. She knew that the jolly little seamstress would be less jolly, probably refuse to acknowledge that she had taken the ring. But Favia was in a fighting mood. She crossed the square in her confident fashion, earning curious looks from the citizenry, who undoubtedly thought it odd that the Kyles could not keep their maidservants better employed.

Her belligerent mood was a trifle weakened when Ma-

182

dame Dureau, rearranging the window, waved and nodded to her as though they were longtime friends and equals.

"You came about your ring," she began before Favia could pour out any threats.

"Yes. I don't wish to sell it, but if I might use it as security for a gown to wear tomorrow night, I should be most grateful."

Madame Dureau clapped her hands, her eyes sparkling. "And so you shall. If I might buy the ring outright, you would profit even more."

"No. I prefer to borrow with the ring as security."

"I quite understand." She bustled around the counter, headed into the unknown recesses at the rear but called back with her bubbling laugh, "This lady, your employer, she must have a real affection for you."

"For me?"

"Such a lavish gift! You did say the ring was a gift?"

"A delightful lady," Favia said firmly, pleased to correct in this moment all the vile things said and thought about her during the last week. "Quite as kind and charming as any lady in England." She added a last fillip, "Kinder."

Madame Dureau seemed unimpressed. "Let me show you what I have in mind. It will suit you to perfection."

Favia did not expect much. She was fully prepared to ask for fresh lengths of material of a more flattering shade and to urge that the woman work all night, if necessary, to get it ready for tomorrow evening. It was the sort of thing she had done uncounted times in the past.

But unusual things had happened in the last week. Everything was different, including herself. All her resolutions to have repairs done were unnecessary. The gown Madame Dureau brought out was exquisite, a blue-silk gauze that matched her eyes so well it might have been chosen deliberately. The undergown was of silk, which shimmered as it caught the light under the transparent gauze. Madame Dureau brought it forward. Favia clapped her hands.

"Enchanting." She felt a pinch of regret that she could not wear her grandmother's diamond parure with this gown. The sapphires would be just slightly off in hue. But in any case, she was reasonably sure she would appear at her best in the gown.

Perhaps Madame Dureau had priced the pearl in the ring and knew its worth. Whatever her reason, she had found a dress remarkably suited to Favia.

"In my parlor I have a looking glass. Come. Let us see what it makes of you, dearie."

It was all very strange to Favia Dalreagh, whose seamstresses invariably came to Dalreagh or the London house to create her wardrobe after long consultations, often in Favia's own sitting room, but never in a London shop. She was learning a deal more than she had ever imagined when she left Brighton.

In Madame Dureau's crowded, overfurnished back parlor with its one small window looking out upon thatched roofs on a lower street, Favia removed her parlor maid's uniform. The gown and undergown proved to be a trifle short, matters that Madame Dureau assured her could be rectified. Otherwise the fit was perfect, and the sight of herself in the seamstress's long mirror was everything she could hope for.

"It was to have been a wedding gown for a young lady from Rye town, but the wedding did not occur. She cried off at the last moment, and here was I, with this lovely gown."

With eyes that could not get enough of the beautiful

creation, Favia told Madame Dureau, "I cannot thank you enough. It is enchanting."

"You are enchanting, miss. Let me carry it to the Kyle house tomorrow." As Favia began to protest, the little woman giggled and added, "Early tomorrow?"

"Wonderful. I am delighted."

Favia returned to the Kyle house across the square in great spirits. She was feeling so exhilarated, she agreed to help Bidlington serve at dinner and made almost no mistakes until the dessert. The dinner itself was not difficult. Miss Selina's only guest was the squire's widow, who spent the entire meal describing the idiosyncrasies of the great lady who had purchased her late husband's stone house above the estuary. When they reached the biscuits à l'orange, the gâteaux and the apple tarts, the widow came to the crux of her gossip.

"So curious, these ladies of title. They would appear to have no sense of morality. The Duchess of Hungerford speaks with such frankness to her guests about the affairs at court, about her friendships and their peculiar jests. She calls the Prince Regent 'Prinny.' And that dreadful Dalreagh woman. How she talks of her! And yet they are popularly supposed to be bosom-bows."

"Dalreagh!" exclaimed Miss Selina, rapping her spoon sharply against her plate. "The name stinks in the nostrils of decent men."

This was a trifle beyond the widow's spoken vocabulary. "My dear Selina!"

"Perfectly true. Ruined my life."

Favia lingered by the windows in a state of keen excitement.

The widow murmured, "Not—the late earl?"

"Late, indeed. By about twenty-three years, I should say."

185

"A jilt? Oh, my dear Selina!"

"The banns were to be published on that Sunday. We had no word. Neither Stephen nor I. My brother was only fifteen. No intimation until the last minute. Simply His Lordship's regrets and the remark that I would understand because ours had not been a love match. He meant, of course, that he had chosen me for my money. To add to the Dalreagh fortune. I was presumably marrying him for his absurd title. As though I cared for such medieval nonsense."

"Oh, dear."

"Quite so. He chose to marry a descendant of the Plantagenets. With not a farthing to bless herself."

'While the widow made *tsk-tsk* sounds, Bidlington summoned Favia, who lingered during her exit, hoping to hear something that would soften the disgusting social crime of her father.

It was difficult to find anything to say on the Earl of Dalreagh's behalf. Favia was sickened by her father's thoughtless cruelty. Selina Kyle had been one of those women who love once and do not forget. Even if she had not been passionately in love with the earl, the humiliation must have been frightful to last this long.

As a woman who had herself fallen desperately in love, Favia could now sympathize with Miss Selina.

It took some minutes for Favia to realize that her father's cold-blooded jilt of Selina Kyle might end, once and for all time, any hope that Stephen would forgive Favia for her deception, the wager, or her parentage.

All her euphoric feelings after seeing herself in Madame Dureau's gown seemed to vanish during the afternoon. She had already learned of Stephen's hatred toward the Dalreaghs. He must remember vividly that time when he was fifteen-years-old and his beloved sister suffered. Perhaps his very youth had made him more sensitive to her pain.

She was still in a turmoil when Cook waved her out of the narrow stillroom pantry where she had stopped to consider the sins of the Dalreaghs. "You there. Girl. Take out the slops. Make yourself of some use while you are about it."

It seemed extraordinary to Favia, considering the homeliness of the task, but she had never before seen table scraps, both sweet and foul, piled into one container, a large, battered old pail, smelling to the skies. She carried the pail out to the marsh steps as ordered, more and more impressed by the long hours and physical labor performed by kitchen workers.

She tossed out the contents of the pail, into the watery marshes below, wondering what creatures would eat the scraps. She was about to go back inside, marveling at the unexpected warmth of the night, which promised good weather for the ball tomorrow, when something struck her cheek. She raised her hand, supposing an insect, or even a small sea bird had flown too close, but she heart the pebble fall to the step and swung around nervously.

At first, she could see nothing in the starlit darkness. The sounds in the marshes were magnified, little sucking noises that gave her mental pictures of those creatures who swam, or prowled all around her. Certainly none of them had thrown the pebble. To the north of the steps there was another noise. Gritting. As though a booted foot had slipped off a rock.

She saw him then. Even in silhouette she recognized the muscular form of the man called Bucko. He signaled to her and called in a hoarse whisper, "Ma'am? Can I speak to you? Quiet-like?"

She peered in the other direction, trying to see whether he might have comrades waiting for him. And for her.

The little beach was deserted. As far as she could make out along the water's edge she and Bucko were alone. She went down the steps until they were only a few feet apart. "What do you wish to say?"

"Firstly, ma'am, there'll be my thanks." His grin made him look almost shy. She saw that he had lost a tooth on the right side of his big, friendly mouth. He did not look like the terror of the seas tonight.

"You tried to help me."

"I never counted to war on females. I tried not to bind you too tight." He added ruefully, "No use anyhow. We fought in your coach. I've seen plenty of blood on a quarterdeck but not like old Maskel and you, ma'am. Not—victims. So, I walked away when we stopped at Hastings."

"You lost nothing in doing so. The woman made off with the profits."

"True, ma'am," he admitted. "That must've been the next morning, from what I gather. That's not what I come to say."

She glanced around again, wondering and suspicious. Still no one in sight. "Perhaps you should say it so that I may trust you."

"Well, then, I hear things. Along this coast, and all. Peeber's still about somewhere."

"I know."

"And since he's lost your treasure, the scuttle is that there's a great lady will make his fortune before he's off to the Continent. And, ma'am, you're the only great lady in his reach." He stood back, scratched his head, and admitted, "Even though a body mightn't recognize you this way, ma'am."

"A jest upon some political friends."

"Aye, ma'am. It's for you to say. I'll be on my way now. But here's thank you again."

She was surprised to see his broad, calloused hand offered to her. She laughed and put her own hand in his. "Here is my gratitude as well."

Seconds later, she hurried up the steps and into the house. She wished Stephen Kyle would return. It seemed to her that even though he did not know of her masquerade, she must be safer if he were here.

She looked around as she entered, but no one seemed to have witnessed her little conversation with the exhighway-man.

She was determined on one thing. Tomorrow night, after the Staff Ball, she would tell Stephen the entire story. There was little likelihood that he might forgive her, but it must be done.

CHAPTER FIFTEEN

Although Favia always awoke early, the noise in the square the next morning was so great it became clearly audible even on the Channel side of the house. By the time she wandered down the servants' stairs to be scolded for the lateness of the hour, Favia could see both males and females, adults and children, frantically active all around the square. Dogs chased cats to produce a further cacophony as the animals ran between the ribbons and tripped up the hard workers.

Beginning with the half-timbered Tudor tavern, which would be the scene of the Staff Ball, every building was decorated with paper streamers and ribbons flying in the salt wind.

In the center of the square the little fountain was transformed. A maypole grew out of what had been the spray, and varicolored ribbons fluttered in every direction, only awaiting the effort to weave them into their silken braids. Favia was used to maypoles during the proper spring festival in the country, but all this festivity held a special enchantment. Much as she feared the outcome of her confession to Stephen, she looked forward to the night's entertainment. And her delightful gown from Madame Dureau, the gown that had been created for a bride who'd cried off her marriage, that, too, might help her in some insidious way.

Why had the bride cried off? Was that a bad omen for the gown?

Before she could dwell too long on these aspects Daniel Mortmain came across the square, headed toward the Kyle house. Seeing Favia, he stopped, made an abrupt right-hand turn, and came to a stand before her. Under his arm he carried a sheaf of thick paper. This was natural for an artist, but what amused Favia was the sight of the long-handled brushes standing straight out of the shot-belt of his jacket, cheek by jowl with pieces of charcoal. Daniel Mortmain did not look like the kind of man who would wear shot-belts for the usual purpose, and Favia smiled to see him.

"You promised to sit for me, Libbie."

"Yes, sir. But I should think the square with all these decorations would be more rewarding."

This struck the artist as a good notion. He decided to combine the two challenges. He seated Favia on the stones that encircled the fountain and arranged several ribbons on the pole so that they fluttered around her, attracting considerable attention from the high-spirited citizens.

The sketch proved to be a good likeness in charcoal, praised by most of the passersby but not by the Duchess of Hungerford, who happened along to advise the busy workers. Her presence in no way reassured Favia. The duchess immediately displayed her malice.

"Ah! the fair abigail. How proud your family must be to know you are in service to a distinguished Member of Parliament! Would you believe, Mr. Mortmain, that this charming creature gave up a post with the Prince Regent.

191

Or as near as makes no matter. Yes. She was my own abigail very briefly."

Daniel Mortmain busied himself with his charcoal, having given her only the vaguest sign that he was listening.

But others nearby gave the duchess some attention. She was well worth looking at that morning, in stark black and white, one of the fuller-skirted gowns with a negligently draped shawl of black hair adorned by a high, black comb. Seeing that she had disturbed Favia, she pursued her advantage.

"As a former, if minor, adornment of the court, are you interested in the latest gossip about Prinny?"

Daniel, seeing something in his subject's face that he read as distaste, chided the duchess mildly, "Perhaps it is respect for our sovereign's person that makes Libbie incurious."

"Prinny is not our sovereign quite yet," the duchess said. "And meanwhile, Beckett, I shouldn't think your new mistress has confided to you that Prinny's entire entourage is involved in a certain matter. Something vulgar about winning a marriage proposal for a wager, I believe. But then, what can one expect from that quarter?"

Daniel cut in, "Excuse me, Your Grace, but in spite of His Highness's sudden change to Tory politics, he still deserves our respect."

The duchess laughed. "Child, what can you mean? The quarter I refer to is the family of Dalreagh."

This was too much for Favia. "The family of Dalreagh made its so-called wager with the Duchess of Hungerford, did it not, Your Grace?"

Daniel cleared his throat in a warning to the abigail that she must take care. Such a challenge made from a serving woman to an aristocrat of Beatrix Hungerford's background might have serious consequences. But he need not have troubled over Favia. The duchess had seen Deborah Mortmain instructing servants in front of the Kyle house as they decorated the ancient walls and the heavily timbered front door. The duchess approached Miss Mortmain.

Favia listened anxiously when she heard Stephen Kyle's name. Deborah's sweetly proprietary attitude about the house seemed to annoy the duchess.

"I trust dear Stephen won't take amiss all your work on his behalf."

Miss Mortmain had no intention of accepting a setdown from this antiquated female. "I have Selina's permission, Your Grace. We are such old friends we know precisely each other's tastes. But there. How would Your Grace know? A stranger in our midst."

While Favia smiled with satisfaction, the duchess pursed her lips, accepting at least one defeat. "Bravo. Well played, Miss Mortmain. But has it occurred to you that your arrows are directed at the wrong target? If you do not take care, you will find you have lost your friend Stephen to a highwayman's doxy."

"A what? I trust I misunderstand you, ma'am."

Her shock was as nothing to Favia's feelings. It took all Daniel's coaxing to keep her looking straight ahead.

"Your trust is misplaced, Miss Mortmain," the duchess assured here. "He may already have discovered the charms of Lemuel Peeber's mistress. Gossip has it that the girl is a beauty who might appear suddenly in any guise. And Stephen Kyle has spent at least twenty-four hours pursuing those who were part of Peeber's gang. Isn't that so?"

Favia was forced to admire Deborah Mortmain's soft laugh and her sublime confidence.

"Dear duchess, you must not judge us here in Sussex by the appalling manners and morals of the Carlton House set. . . . Peter, the white ribbons from that window latch. The blue from the lintel. About here, I think."

The duchess rapped Miss Mortmain's knuckles with one strong, fleshy forefinger. "Be wise, my dear. Make yourself more accessible to your Stephen. Be loving and attentive. Hover. He has a taste for the maternal in women. Behave as the ladies at court behave with him. I have seen him quite swept away by— But enough of this. What a fool I am to waste good advice upon you, of all women!"

She sauntered away over the cobblestones, leaving Favia appalled at her advice, which showed so little understanding of Stephen Kyle. Favia glanced at Deborah Mortmain. That lady frowned, appeared to be deep in thought. No doubt, she was turning over in her mind the advice of a woman who knew Stephen so well.

Belatedly Favia grinned.

The artist lowered his charcoal. "Something amuses you, Libbie?"

"Nothing, sir. A little private jest."

It would be less humorous tonight when everything between Stephen and Favia very probably came to an end.

Daniel Mortmain completed his sketch in time to show it to Stephen when he came striding up Darking Hill from the stables. Favia had been called in to the house by Bidlington and ordered to "make ready" the dining room, but she managed to watch Stephen walk in with Daniel Mortmain.

She hoped and feared at the same time. She was haunted by the thought of what Stephen might have learned during his interrogation of the Dover tapster. He had not yet seen her when he took the big, flimsy paper from the artist and set it up with the board behind it propped against the epergne and stepped back to study the picture in the manner of a connoisseur.

"A speaking portrait," he announced after considerable thought. "What do you ask for it?"

Favia had lost interest in the likeness. She was too enthralled by Stephen Kyle himself as he stood across the room from her. She watched his straight, trim back. He still wore the fawn-colored, many-caped greatcoat and top boots of a traveler. The greatboat was worn loose, and he probably would be glad of a bath and change after his long ride. But he remained to bargain for the portrait.

Surely he would not care to own the portrait if he had learned something disastrous about her.

The proud artist was embarrassed. "I had rather not, Stephen. I mean to say, I think it suggests my best charcoal work, and I should like to keep it as a memento of—of my advance."

"Your advance."

"As an artist."

"Of course." Stephen was admirably grave. "And you will not part with it?"

"I should prefer not to do so."

Unable to keep silent longer, Favia moved away from her corner, making the eager suggestion, "Perhaps Mr. Daniel would do another sketch, sir." Stephen turned to look at her without smiling, almost without seeming to notice her. "I mean," she hurried on, "as an example of Mr. Daniel's skill."

Stephen ignored her part in the suggestion. He slapped his riding gloves into his other hand, said briskly, "We'll discuss it another time. Now if you will excuse me, I'll be shaking off some of the dust of the road. Do we all meet at the tavern tonight?"

Daniel's enthusiasm poured out. "I should rather think so! And Stephen, you may as well know: I shall ask your Libbie Beckett for the German Waltz."

"Certainly. Certainly." Stephen brushed the matter off with an ease that was painful to Favia. He took the artist's arm and escorted him out of the room, still complaining about the dust of the road.

Knowing what I went through at Peeber's hands, she thought angrily, *the least he might do is relieve my mind about whatever he learned.*

On the other hand there was always the strong possibility that he had decided the description of Peeber's female partner in crime fitted "Libbie Beckett" much too well. This was as horrifying as any discovery he might make.

Long before dusk every household in the Cinque Ports was alive with unaccustomed excitement. Whereas, in the general way of things, ladies' maids hurried up and down stairs with hipbaths and long bundles of sparkling silk, spurred on by the impatient cries of their mistresses, tonight the reverse was true. Servants of every age and degree stood nervously while their employers dressed them, some with elegance, but more often, with an overabundance of finery.

No one looked more like a pompous and terrifying Lord Mayor of London than the butler Bidlington. In the upper hall he offered his arm gallantly to the stout cook. Though sweating as usual, she radiated splendor in crimson velvet and satin. The door of Favia's room remained open while Miss Selina limped in accompanied by the maid who had attended Favia two days ago and the beaming Madame Dureau, with her great bundle wrapped in silver paper and draped over her arms. Through that open door, Favia saw Bidlington and the cook pass by, the latter casting a triumphant smile in Favia's direction.

"It is very festive," Favia remarked more brightly than she felt.

She let the three women dress her, since they drew much

196

pleasure from it, and since her dining room encounter with Stephen had proved so unsatisfactory. It would be hard to say which woman enjoyed it most. Miss Selina was absurdly masquerading as a cook in a stained pinafore over an old calico gown, with her dark-blond hair hidden beneath an unfrilled white bonnet. Her maid, on the contrary, wore a resplendent brocade gown of the previous century, complete with panniers that somewhat limited her activities. Madame Dureau was a saucy little soubrette. She looked like a charming flirt.

They were all pleased by Favia's appearance in the blue-silk gauze with her hair perfectly arranged and the picture completed by white silk slippers, which fitted her surprisingly well. The gown itself fitted superbly, although Miss Selina grumbled that the deep-cut square neck was far too low, and that it was a pity "Libbie Beckett" 's bosom was so high and well-rounded.

"The gown makes the most of it," she sighed. "I daresay, you might conceal them—it—by your shawl, but heavens! The shawl itself is practically transparent." Favia looked down and was amused. The spider-web white lace was not very useful as a concealing wrap, but luckily the evening was still warm.

Critically she regarded herself in the looking glass, feeling naked without jewelry until Miss Selina brought out a necklace of small, perfectly matched diamonds identical to the dangling earrings she and the maid had fastened to Favia's earlobes. A fine spray of diamonds set in Favia's hair displayed her short, curly coiffure perfectly in the Grecian mode.

"I wore the set at my presentation to Their Majesties twenty-four years ago. Guard them well, my girl," she warned Favia, who was touched by the loan of such precious objects.

"I shall, ma'am, I promise you. I am so very grateful."

Gratitude. A curious new lesson to her; one of many.

Miss Selina gazed at her as though studying her. "This is a trust, Libbie Beckett. I have demonstrated my faith in the honesty of others and occasionally been disappointed. There are some that think me a fool. Are you one of them?"

Favia felt the prick of tears. She could not remember when a stranger had trusted her without knowing her true background. She sniffed, smiled tremulously, and promised, "I will guard them with my life and return them safely to your hands."

Miss Selina patted her roughly. "Good. And you will have our friend Daniel to guard you. He was going to Rye, but I am persuaded the fellow will keep his promise and meet you belowstairs, or on the doorstep. I expect he is in the square even now, picturing how the festivities will look on canvas. Run along. Glance out into the square. He is sure to be on the watch."

Numb with anxiety, Favia was pushed out into the hall, urged to go down, find Daniel Mortmain, and join the laughing, shouting throng in the square. She thought, I feel as if I were making my first entry up the old staircase to Almack's and wondering if any gentleman will possibly see in me a dancing partner. She straightened her shoulders. She had eventually conquered Almack's sacred rooms, and she was being given one more chance to conquer her blunders and mistakes tonight.

Contrary to her secret hope, she did not find Stephen Kyle waiting at the foot of the stairs to escort her across the square. More surprisingly, neither was the artist in sight.

She stepped out into the square, trying to find Daniel Mortmain in that tangled, laughing mass of villagers. He must be somewhere among them. She was assailed by nerve-racking memories as she made her way among these people who looked less friendly and innocent at this hour. The torches flaring from every building around the square only added to the unreal quality of the setting. Nor was she reassured when a French fisherman in wide-legged pantaloons and a striped shirt was thrust against her by the chain of dancers around the fountain maypole.

She found herself looking into the eyes of "Bucko," the ex-seaman. She should not have been surprised. She knew he was somewhere hereabouts, but the sight of him suggested that, like his sudden appearance, she might also find Lemuel Peeber looking into her eyes. Lemuel Peeber might hold her to ransom, like a pirate on the Spanish Main.

"Lady Favia," the seaman began, breathing fast. "I've been on the watch for you."

She looked around hurriedly. "Please. Not yet. I am still 'Libbie Beckett.' Why are you here?"

"Well, ma'am, I might be swinging from a gibbet this minute but for you, so I thought I'd just drift about tonight to be at hand, so to speak, if Peeber takes a fancy to trouble you."

She was touched and gave him her hand. "You are very good, Captain—Bucko."

"Buckhurst, that's the name of this old barque. And many thanks again."

The dancers were all around them, and he let himself be swallowed up in their midst. The night breeze had begun to flutter the ribbons of the maypole, and these, along with the flare of the torches, disguised every face in the crowd. She wondered if any of these unknown creatures in fancy dress could be Lemuel Peeber. Confused and trying to decide whether to go on alone, she moved toward the tavern at the head of the steep main street.

The dancers in the square were keeping time to the music, which was clearly audible through the open doors of the tavern. Violins scraped joyously, and a pianoforte was played with more emphasis than skill. Favia found her feet tapping to the music.

The country airs so popular during the last half hour came to a squeaking, off-key stop. The dancers swung away, looking toward the open tavern doors, where the golden light from the lamps within poured out upon the cobblestones. To Favia's surprise, when the music swelled up again, it was one of the shocking and sensuous new waltzes brought over from the Continent in the wake of the Napoleonic Wars.

Several local residents poured into the tavern, but one man walked out against the tide and headed across the street toward her. Stephen Kyle looked exactly as she had pictured him, in his correct evening attire, but not in costume, exactly the way he had looked long ago at the Bath Assembly when he snubbed a seventeen-year-old girl waiting nervously for her first partner. She had not yet made her come-out in London and would certainly not have danced the daring waltz without the sanction of Almack's patronesses. But his indifference had been a severe blow to her pride and her schoolgirl infatuation with him.

After all those years it appeared that he was going to rectify the error he had committed in Bath. He held out his hands. She curtsied as low as her skirts would allow. She wondered if the glitter in his eyes was the reflection of her gown and jewels, which had caught the torchlight.

He slipped one hand around her waist, and his other hand closed over hers. She pretended to look around.

"Where is Master Daniel?"

"I persuaded him the town council at Rye wished to buy one of his marine landscapes."

"And do they?"

He grinned. "Of course they do. What do you take me for? A liar?"

That left her self-consciously silent, remembering her own sins in that field.

"You are in very good looks tonight, Miss Beckett," he told her, and swung her out to the music. It was hardly an enthusiastic compliment, but she was grateful for any kind words from him.

"You are too kind, sir."

"Not at all. You perform your tasks tolerably well."

She laughed. "So, the noble M.P. is capable of an untruth."

"I?" That raised his eyebrows.

"I am the worst parlor maid in Sussex."

"Ah," he amended smoothly. "But you do what is required of you in the kitchen, according to Cook. With training, I think you may do very well as a scullery maid."

She played his game, forgetting "Libbie Beckett."

"What an odious creature you are!"

The muscles of his arm tightened around her waist. He was swinging her so rapidly in the turn that she almost slipped on the uneven cobbles. He held her to him with that same firmness. She was not entirely sure he meant to tease her when he said, "Odious, am I? Then, it shouldn't matter what I do, an odious fellow like me."

Before she could make a reply his lips were hard upon hers, and she found herself effectively silenced. She was much too sophisticated to play the outraged young maiden. Instead she yielded to the feeling that his kiss excited in her and returned it with all the passion she had repressed so long. The touch of him and his possession of her filled her with elation. He returned her love. She knew it now. Surely he would understand about the masquerade. Later.

201

Absurdly enough, she realized they were still moving slowly in the dance, though they clung together in that breathless kiss, neither willing to bring the moment to an end. Around them, a few women giggled, but others were behaving with the same abandon, and it wasn't until his name was called sharply, in the voice of a stern governess, that they separated.

He looked around, demanded coolly, "Who called me?"

Sounding quite unlike herself, Deborah Mortmain tapped his shoulder. "Stephen, I must speak to you."

"Another time."

"It is important. A pair of excisemen are here to see you. They have found the coach and horses abandoned near Rye by the murderers of that innkeeper, Jude Maskel. No one knows what happened to the owner of the carriage."

He released Favia's body slowly. "How do they know they are the same coach and horses?"

"It seems they took up two of the highwaymen, thinking they were smugglers. The rogues confessed."

He looked at Favia. "I will be needed." To Deborah, he asked, still in the administrator's tone he used toward her tonight, "How did you happen to find out all this?"

She was very much upon her mettle. "I was waiting at Kyle House for you to escort me to the festivities, when they came to find you. The excise officers will meet you in the private parlor of the tavern. You will find the highwaymen in the old French Jailhouse at the foot of the hill."

"The French Jailhouse. That antiquated dungeon? Good God! Do they intend a hanging in the courtyard without a trial? Very well. I'll be on my way." He stared at Favia in a curious manner, with a tinge of sadness that dismayed her. "Wait at the house."

"Yes, sir."

He started away from her. Miss Mortmain followed. Favia could not miss the woman's satisfaction as she reminded him, "I have not told you the whole of it. The highwaymen insist that this Peeber's female accomplice is the real thief. The most dangerous member of the gang. A woman named Libbie Beckett."

While Favia remained there, stiff with dread, Stephen strode across the square, waving away the company of Deborah Mortmain. With dragging feet Favia made her way through the happy, drunken throng toward the Kyle house. As she passed the dark little alley behind the north wall that led down a dusty path to the marshes, she saw some movement in the blackness and took a quick step backward.

The bright, cutting blade of a seaman's dirk flashed before her. Lemuel Peeber, of course. Shaken but furious, she cried out. A second later the blade was at her throat. The sound of her scream was drowned by the noise of the crowd.

The now bearded cutthroat muttered, "This time, you'll serve me proper, my girl. You just might be worth more to me than all your gewgaws." One of his hands covered her mouth, and the other held the lengthy edge of the dirk steady against her bare throat. She bit down with all her strength but failed to do more than taste the salt and sweat of his palm. He brought his knee hard up against her stomach, and she sank to her knees, choking, feeling herself dragged into the little alley.

She stumbled over a man lying huddled against the wall of the Kyle house and groaned at the contact. Peeber was still trying to drag her along, but she resisted, grasping at the ground, the wall, then the man's slack hand. The sea wind made a nearby torch in the square flare up. She made out the striped shirt and pantaloons, and the battered face, of Captain Buckhurst.

CHAPTER SIXTEEN

For an instant she thought he was dead, but under her frantic prowling fingers she felt his labored breathing. Thank heaven for that!

"Get to your feet, you baggage!" Peeber's command was low but perfectly audible. He shook her arm. "Get up! And while we're about it, let's have them pretty sparkles around your neck. How did Libbie miss them?"

"Don't touch them. They are not mine." She struggled to free herself. She managed to keep the necklace, which proved difficult to break. He cuffed her across the throat, cursing.

"I'll be getting it. Don't you fret about that."

Out in the square the scene had grown noisier. Running feet. Laughter and shouts. Favia got up with difficulty, but she knew that if she failed to arouse anyone now, she might never have another opportunity. She threw her weight against Peeber to knock him off balance, but he was ready for her and raised the dirk.

At the same time something very like a stormcloud struck Peeber. Favia heard the hideous crunch of bone and flesh. Stephen Kyle dragged Peeber up by one arm, shook him, then threw him down again, turning to Favia. "Are you hurt?"

She shook her head, too hoarse to speak.

He returned to the groaning Peeber, asking the excise officer behind him, "Is this the creature we are after?"

The little officer peered into the alley. "You seemed mighty bent on saving that doxy. Aye, this'll be Peeber, right enough. Lucky you saw them two fighting-like. Who's the dead laddie?"

Favia struggled with her voice. She managed a whisper. "A man named Buckhurst. Tried to save me. Please help him."

The little man got a whining, grunting Peeber to his feet and hustled him out to the square while the cutthroat complained that his arm was "busted-sure." The officer looked back at Stephen, who was examining the unconscious Bucko. "Will you be bringing along the doxy? She's our wench, and no mistake. Peeber must've been trying to get out of her where she hid the jewels and such."

Favia tried to protest. "No. Not like that. You don't understand." She saw Stephen examining Bucko with a businesslike efficiency. "Stephen, is he—?"

"A bad knock across the head. Face is bruised. Probably a kick or two." Stephen reached for Bucko's body, slung the seaman over his shoulder, and stood up, balancing the load with an ease that Favia admired, even in these moments of her own dread.

Stephen gave her a long, hard look. "Go with Lieutenant Gavin. I'll be along as soon as I've put this rogue in someone's care."

She tried to begin her explanation once more, but Lieutenant Gavin of His Majesty's Excise Service waved her on before him with his heavy pistol, whose barrel fascinated Lemuel Peeber.

"You are making a great error," Favia warned the lieutenant. "I am not the—the doxy you think I am. I happen to be Lady Favia Dalreagh."

"Happy to make your acquaintance, ma'am. Run along ahead, ma'am. But not too far."

Since she shared Peeber's mistrust of the pistol and saw that the officer was too stupid to reason with, she obeyed him. She had never before objected to appearing conspicuous, but to walk down an ancient cobbled street late at night in a ball gown and only a fine lace shawl was more than she had bargained for. The entire village seemed to have stopped their laughter and dancing in order to watch this party of criminals.

Once Lemuel Peeber lurched against her, and she saw his knowing smirk. She looked quickly at the lieutenant, but that worthy was on the watch and jabbed the highwayman so painfully in the small of the back that Peeber momentarily lost interest in an escape.

Favia tried to convince herself that as soon as Stephen arrived he would explain things and all must go well. Perhaps it had happened for the best. When he realized how much she had suffered tonight, he would be happy to forgive her.

This optimism lasted until she saw the interior of the French Jailhouse, a sinister-looking stone edifice of a single story, built on the border of the marshes, whose floor appeared to be somewhat below the level of the mud and reeds, not to mention the water's edge and any inquisitive sheep. From its name she assumed the jail had been built in earlier centuries to house French raiders or smugglers.

Favia did not know whether to be relieved or more terrified when she was separated from Lemuel Peeber, and a husky exciseman rode off with him manacled in a cart, to what was probably a larger and more secure prison until his trial and hanging.

Favia was shoved before little Lieutenant Gavin into the guardroom of the ancient jail. There was a bench along one wall, even more uncomfortable than an unpadded settle, for it had no back. Felons and their witnesses, and probably their visitors, must sit there. A huge oaken desk took up much of the remaining space at one end of the room and was impressive enough to frighten any criminal (or otherwise) into a confession. No one sat there at the moment, and she regained hope.

She tried once more to reason with Lieutenant Gavin or the gap-toothed farmer lad who seemed to be cleaning out the guardroom and stared at her as if she were someone from far Cathay.

"I am the Lady Favia Dalreagh. Anyone who has an acquaintance with His Highness or the court will recognize me. Surely, there is some witness you might bring. From Rye perhaps. Or Hastings."

"Or Darking Hill?"

She missed the irony. "I can't think of anyone at the moment. But there must be someone."

The lieutenant bestowed a knowing grin on the lad with the broom-straws and the pail of water. "If you were what you claim to be, you would know that we have in Darking Hill a very particular friend to His Highness, yet you didn't name Her Grace, the Duchess of Hungerford."

Beatrix Hungerford would be only too glad to testify in Favia's behalf and at the same time, win their wager, that awful wager Favia had never been able to crush. "Yes. I had forgotten. Do ask Her Grace to come. She will do."

The lieutenant shrugged. "And in the meantime, I suggest Your Highness get a good rest. You'll be fair busy tomorrow, what with being brought up before the justice

207

and sentenced for theft and murder, and by the by, the disappearance of Her Ladyship, Lady Favia Dalreagh. It seems she was waylaid by highwaymen and hasn't been seen since.''

She was much too desperate to worry about pride. She tried to shake his sleeve in her anxiety. "Just ask Stephen Kyle to hurry. He will know what to do.''

"He's busy right now. Howsoever, we'll see.'' He kicked open the heavy door at the opposite end of the room.

Still protesting in a fury that had reached panic, Favia was hurried into the narrow passage in front of what appeared to be two cells, stone-walled, with iron-reinforced doors. She had committed the indignity of struggling at the last minute, and the lieutenant needed the help of the farm-boy before they got her locked into the cell. They slammed shut the door with a metallic clang that seemed to pierce Favia's body like the dirk Stephen had twisted out of Pee-ber's hand.

The place was not quite dark, thanks to the starry night above the barred window. Wisps of fog had dissolved, and Favia stared around her at the cell. There was a pail of water in one corner and a three-legged stool. Nothing else. No one seemed to have noticed or cared that the tidal water seeped in to cover the stone floor. During high tides and storms prisoners would be lucky not to drown if they were caught asleep on the floor.

Stephen Kyle must save her. Surely he would.

She stretched and tried to smooth out the wrinkles in the once-lovely gauze and silk of her gown. Then she stepped up on the stool and looked out.

The view was not encouraging. An ancient gibbet stood in the narrow earthen courtyard. Beyond a low wall the marshes encroached, thick as an impenetrable swamp. So, this was the end for wretches like Libbie Beckett.

. . . I might have been a Libbie Beckett. What separates me from them? Only my parents and my ancestors. And, long ago, a robber baron who befriended William the Conqueror. . . .

She jumped down from the stool when she heard heavy, booted footsteps in the stone passage. The door clanged open, grating across the floor. She saw the farmboy holding a storm lantern as Lieutenant Gavin pushed him aside and entered the cell. He had already taken her arm and was hustling her out toward the guardroom before she could make any more indignant protests.

Recovering as they entered the guardroom, she tried to make him understand in a breathless rush of words, "I'm not really that creature. Please believe me. It was Mister Kyle who assumed I was Libbie Beckett. Ask the Duchess of Hungerford. We are old friends."

She was still talking when she blinked in the light of a lamp and several lanterns and discovered she was appearing disheveled, hair uncombed, her shawl hugged to her bosom, before several witnesses. For all the world like a common doxy, she thought despairingly.

She saw Stephen first, sitting behind the huge desk and watching her, unsmiling. Lieutenant Gavin stood beside him, leaving her unattended. Even the farmboy watched from a corner, having set down the lantern and taken up his bundle of broom-straws. His blue eyes were wide and wondering.

Most humiliating to her was the sight of Selina Kyle, looking stern as ever and seated very erect on the hard bench. Her big, plain travel cloak failed to cover the front panel of the absurd pinafore she had worn in her masquerade as a cook. She must have come here very rapidly to view the punishment of Lemuel Peeber's doxy.

Favia felt that the blood of the Dalreaghs demanded no

less than a display of pride now. She unfastened the necklace. One of the earrings had caught in her tangled hair. She jerked it off with the other and, together with the handful of neat, unostentatious diamonds, held them out to Selina. "Whatever may be said of me, madam, I am not a thief. I intended to return them."

Selina said harshly, "So I should imagine." She dropped the jewels into an inner pocket of her cloak and sat watching Favia. Strangely enough, it seemed to Favia that her taut mouth trembled in a brief second or two, then the thin lips pressed tight together.

She knows, thought Favia, deeply moved by the knowledge that this good-hearted woman must despise her, and only partly for her father.

Stephen's voice brought her to attention. "Lieutenant Gavin tells me you claim to be a certain Favia Dalreagh, daughter of the late earl. You asked that Her Grace, the Duchess of Hungerford, testify in your behalf. The lady obliged. She went to the trouble of having her chair-boys bring her here. Gavin, ask if she will step inside."

"And tell my own chair-boys to wait," his sister added. "I will not be long."

With her heart beating fast, Favia watched the door. The duchess swept in. No other word could describe her entrance in black taffeta and a shining comb covered by a magnificent mantilla. Favia gave Stephen Kyle a sideglance. Though he looked severe, she thought his eyes were amused. It was a combination that had attracted her from the first. She hoped that it was a good sign.

"Your Grace is, I believe, familiar with the court of His Highness, the Prince Regent."

"Perfectly true, Stephen—" She coughed delicately. "Dear me, I mean to say—Mr. Kyle." With distaste Selina made room for her on the bench, but the duchess remained standing.

"Then, will you be so good as to identify this person?"

The duchess considered Favia, who burst out impatiently, "You may speak, Beatrix. I give you permission."

"But—" The great lady was all bewilderment. "How can I speak? Do you suggest we are acquainted?"

Lieutenant Gavin interpreted Her Grace's dilemma. "The young person claims she is a certain Lady Favia Dalreagh."

The duchess raised a hand to her full, red lips. "But I would certainly recognize Her Ladyship. We are old friends. Even to a little wager in which His Royal Highness holds a financial interest. It concerns Her Ladyship's betrothal. Of course, this person may know whether I have won or not. If so—" She shrugged, waiting for Favia to speak, but all Favia's Dalreagh pride forbade it.

"That woman is nothing but a common blackmailer."

Probably Selina Kyle had never heard the word before but understood and turned to stare at the duchess.

Stephen dismissed Her Grace. "You may go."

It had come so abruptly, the woman was stunned. Lieutenant Gavin bowed and waved her out. She was so surprised, she went. At the door she looked as though she might change her mind. Then she went on, passing in the doorway a seaman whose head was wrapped in stained linen. She paid him no heed and was soon gone.

Favia was delighted to see Captain Buckhurst, though he looked especially pale for a seafaring man. It seemed clear that he was only just recovering from the attack by Lemuel Peeber, but he had come, all the same.

"Captain," Favia said, wishing her voice did not sound so desperate, "tell them I am not a member of Peeber's cutthroats."

211

Bucko swayed slightly, and both Stephen and the lieutenant reached out to help him, but he waved them away.
"I was at Jude's inn that night, Mr. Stephen, like I told
you. I'd come on bad times, with my ship foundering off
Cape Gris-Nez and the wife being took sick and all. But I
swear to God I never knew they'd kill no one."

"The lady," Stephen reminded him. "I mean—the
young woman. Who is she?"

"Oh. Her." Bucko grinned. "Well, she did me a kind-
ness. It was sort of both ways around. Anyway, she's the
lady that Peeber and his doxy robbed. The Lady Favia
Dalreagh."

The big, chill guardroom was silent. Then someone gave
a heavy sigh. The sound came from Selina Kyle. Favia
reached for the bench and sank down beside her, exhausted. Stephen thanked Bucko and ordered the lieutenant, "Get him to the tavern and to bed. I'll talk to him
tomorrow."

"Is he to be remanded, sir?"

Stephen shook his head. "He did us a great service, and
he twice saved the Lady Favia. Then, too, he is not in your
jurisdiction, since you have not taken him as a smuggler."

The lieutenant looked doubtfully from Bucko to Favia.
"Nor the lady neither?"

"Nor the lady neither."

Stephen reached for a blue, ribbed silk, pelisse on the
back of his chair and held it out to Favia while the lieutenant went out with Bucko, still looking as if he had somehow been compromised in his job.

Favia realized the pelisse was her own. It had been in
her luggage when she had departed from Brighton. Libbie
Beckett must have left it in the coach upon abandoning
Peeber. She fumbled with the sleeves, trying to get the silk
coat on. Suddenly she wanted to cry when Selina reached

out to help her find the armhole. The older woman had not relaxed, but the simple, motherly gesture went to Favia's heart.

She was shocked, however, when Selina said, "Don't snivel. I detest sniveling."

Favia pulled herself together. "I beg your pardon. I must stop Beatrix. It began as a stupid joke. But I have a debt to pay."

Stephen and his sister spoke together. He asked sharply, "You acknowledge the debt?"

Selina said, "Be quiet, Stephen." And to Favia, "If you wish to return to your mother, you need not be troubled over her. "The *on-dit* is that the Dowager Countess of Dalreagh will marry some well-sprung mushroom from the City, Julius Worthingham, by name. I am told he dotes on her."

"Good heavens!" How little Favia and her mother had known each other! She recalled suddenly that the Dowager Countess and Mr. Worthingham had gotten on very well at Dalreagh. As Selina said, he had seemed to dote on her, and the Dowager Countess was certainly born to be the wife of a wealthy man.

Selina Kyle added cynically, "So much for the grieving widow of the man who—" She broke off. "There were others who loved him better." Then she cleared her throat. "But no matter. Until my brother told me an hour ago, I had no notion who you were. I will not trouble you with my feelings in the matter. If my brother believes you have suffered enough, I am prepared to agree."

She got up and limped to the door. She did not shake off Favia's arm when the younger woman tried to help her.

Favia watched her leave. She had never more bitterly regretted the deception. Selina got into her sedan chair, and the youths took up the poles. Then she leaned out and

213

called to her brother, "You could do worse, I daresay. There was once a time when I very much wanted a Dalreagh in the family. So we are merely a trifle delayed." Her bearers trotted away into the starry night.

Favia turned to Stephen, who stood quietly behind her. Anger mingled with deep relief. She realized that he had been unsurprised by the revelation of her real name. "Did you know all the time that I was Favia Dalreagh?"

The impossible man grinned at her, the first softening of his magisterial manner in the last two hours. "Since you have been at Darking Hill, yes. The night I found you at Jude Maskel's told me a good deal. This Dalreagh ring fitted you much too well to be borrowed." He held it out to her in the palm of his hand. She snatched it up angrily and forced it on. He went on as though they were in excellent charity with each other. "There was your manner. Everything about you. I was a fool not to guess in Brighton. Or even at the Dalreagh estate."

He had committed an outrage far worse than her ridiculous wager. She would never forgive him! "Then, all my fear and degradation and suffering were for nothing."

"To the contrary. They paid you in your own coin for that wager. You might have ended what you call your 'degradation' long ago, if you hadn't been so stubborn."

"You mean that all this was my fault?"

"Wasn't it? You persisted in playing the role. I hoped a dozen times that you would tell me the truth. When I kissed you, I knew from your response that your feelings were genuine. I am not always a complete dolt."

"Or a trickster. You tortured me."

"You tortured yourself." His hands were strong and warm upon her shoulders, his lips tantalizingly near her disheveled hair. "I confess, I also thought that if your masquerade proved unpleasant, you might acquire a little un-

214

derstanding of classes other than your own." It was true. He had certainly accomplished that with his mistreatment of her.

He seemed determined to dwell upon all her faults. "But we still have a bit of unfinished business. There is your wager with Her Grace."

"I shall certainly pay it. If I never pay another debt, that must be paid."

He considered this view of the matter, as though it were the merest commonplace. "And yet, why should you? You have won." She started, wondering if she was going to be tiresome and weep again. His voice was unexpectedly gentle. "Come now. Selina will be expecting us back soon, to satisfy the proprieties. And Deborah, too."

"Deborah?"

"My old friend Deborah was responsible for your rescue from that cutthroat. I was with Lieutenant Gavin outside the tavern when Deborah saw you struggling in that alley and called my attention to it in her delightful way. If I recall, she said: 'There goes your precious Libbie Beckett with her paramour.' "

She was outraged. He silenced her fury with his lips. After a brief struggle, she responded with all her heart.

The cleaning boy murmured plaintively, "Will-e be a-needin' of me, sor?"

Without looking around Stephen waved him away. "Lock up and go home. I shall personally take this prisoner in charge."

True romance is <u>not</u> hard to find... you need only look as far as FAWCETT BOOKS

Available at your bookstore or use this coupon.

____	THE FALSE BETHROTHAL, Clarice Peters	20513	2.25
____	SAMANTHA, Clarice Peters	20217	2.25
____	THEA, Clarice Peters	20696	2.50
____	A VERY SIMPLE SCHEME, Rebecca Baldwin	50274	1.50
____	A SEASON ABROAD, Rebecca Baldwin	50215	1.50

FAWCETT MAIL SALES
Dept. TAF, 201 E. 50th St., New York, N.Y. 10022

Please send me the FAWCETT BOOKS I have checked above. I am en-
_sing $....................(add 50¢ per copy to cover postage and handling).
_d check or money order—no cash or C.O.D.'s please. Prices and
_nbers are subject to change without notice. Valid in U.S. only. All orders
_ subject to availability of books.

Name_____

Address_____

City_____State_____Zip Code_____

Allow at least 4 weeks for delivery.   **TAF-43**